Isabel in Bloom

ALSO BY MAE RESPICIO

Any Day with You

How to Win a Slime War

The House That Lou Built

Isabel in Bloom

MAE RESPICIO

WENDY
LAMB
BOOKS

To my grandmothers, Rosa and Dionicia,
whose bountiful gardens I always keep with me

Text copyright © 2024 by Mae Respicio
Jacket art copyright © 2024 by Gica Tam

All rights reserved. Published in the United States by Wendy Lamb Books, an imprint of Random House Children's Books, a division of Penguin Random House LLC, New York.

Wendy Lamb Books and the colophon are trademarks of Penguin Random House LLC.

Visit us on the Web! rhcbooks.com

Educators and librarians, for a variety of teaching tools, visit us at RHTeachersLibrarians.com

Library of Congress Cataloging-in-Publication Data
Names: Respicio, Mae, author.
Title: Isabel in bloom / Mae Respicio.
Description: First edition. | New York : Wendy Lamb Books, 2024. | Audience: Ages 8–12. | Audience: Grades 4–6. | Summary: Making friends in a new city, and new country, is hard for twelve-year-old Isabel, but joining the gardening and cooking club at school helps her find her way.
Identifiers: LCCN 2023004696 (print) | LCCN 2023004697 (ebook) | ISBN 978-0-593-30271-2 (hardcover) | ISBN 978-0-593-30272-9 (lib. bdg.) | ISBN 978-0-593-30273-6 (ebook)
Subjects: CYAC: Novels in verse. | Self-actualization—Fiction. | Family life—Fiction. | Clubs—Fiction. | Gardening—Fiction. | Cooking—Fiction. | Middle schools—Fiction. | Schools—Fiction. | Filipino Americans—Fiction. | LCGFT: Novels in verse.
Classification: LCC PZ7.5.R47 Is 2024 (print) | LCC PZ7.5.R47 (ebook) | DDC [Fic]—dc23

The text of this book is set in 11.3-point Maxime Pro.
Flower bouquet art by lilett/stock.adobe.com
Interior design by Cathy Bobak

Printed in the United States of America
10 9 8 7 6 5 4 3 2 1
First Edition

SEED

HOME

I walk with my grandfather
through
      a thousand shades of green
      plants dressed in dew
      flowers flooded in light
as birds fill the trees with their
wild loud songs.
Our garden
comes alive
in mornings.

Lolo drags a hose
the water trickling slow.
We pause at a planter of

Jasmine
      Sampaguita.

Weeks ago when I found out
I'd have to say goodbye
he made me plant it
So when you return
you'll see how it's grown, he said.

Jasmine
      Sampaguita

takes up most of this space.
Rows of shrubs like fences
small white flowers

perfuming the air with their
sweet lush musk.

But we hover over mine
concerned
leaves wilted
brittle brown stems.
No blossoms here.

I crouch down.
>   *What's wrong, little Jazzy?*
>   I ask, almost expecting a reply.

Plants respond to humans
our voice, our love.
It's why I name and talk to some of ours:
Elvis Parsley and Vincent van Grow,
my favorite, the Spice Girls
(a cluster of herbs named after
a music group my friends and I
dance to when we play our CDs).
>   *Should I have grown it in the ground?*
>   *Or in a different pot?*
>   *Or . . . something?*
>   I ask my grandfather.
>   I don't know what to do.

You should trust.
It's just a little thirsty.

Jasmine
>   Sampaguita

has gifted
my family
our livelihood
by learning the art
of growing and selling.
Its blooms are our survival.

I know its petals
soft and white.
I know its smell
without it near
but I don't know
why this one looks
how I feel
—homesick
heartsick—
when I haven't even
left for California yet.

I sigh.

Feeling nervous for your trip, Isabel?

  If I don't like it there, can I come home?

To my surprise he nods.
But only for visits.

Tricked!

Lolo raises my chin
so our eyes meet.

Sumpa kita
sounds like sampaguita.
It stands for
I promise you.
And I promise
you will do fine
in your new home.

He lays the hose
slips it a drip
saying something
I've already heard
many times, my whole life.

We bloom
where we
are planted.

DON'T WANT TO SAY IT

Goodbyes look like
summer in my small town
green hills and rice fields
my best friends and I strolling toward home.

Goodbyes sound like
chattering about school and friends
how next year we all turn thirteen
—though they'll be here and I'll be elsewhere.

Goodbyes taste like
tart calamansi from Lolo's tree
round, small, and green that Lola's
slicing and squeezing into drinks

for me, Cristina, and Rosamie.

Ice clinks
glasses sweat
we take slow sips
and our lips pucker
from the sweet and the sour.

Goodbyes smell like
sampaguita flowers
Lola's picked and strung
piled high on the table in soft pearly mounds.

Bye, Lola! See you tomorrow, Isabel! my friends say.

Lola waves back and drapes
a single jasmine garland
around my neck the way she does
with each fresh batch.

Goodbye is
Lola's sad smile
the waning sun
that citrus still on my tongue
these white blooms near my heart
her warm hand on my cheek
knowing how much
I already hate saying

goodbye.

ME, ISABEL LIGAYA, AGE TWELVE

I've never lived in a city

I've never seen snow

I've never been rich

I've never had a mother take me to a mall.

I've never left the Philippines

or ridden in an airplane

or wanted to make new best friends

because

I love the ones I already have.

LUNCHTIME

On my last day at school
I sit with Cristina and Rosamie
at our normal spot
under the giant balete tree,
its thick gnarled knots sunk deep
making me wonder
what engkantos and tree fairies
might live there.

I take out my normal lunch
rice and meat
juice, a cookie
and Rosamie takes out
something wrapped with a ribbon.

Open it!

Inside
a beaded bracelet
with three dangly hearts.

Those hearts are us
so you don't forget
your best friends.

They hold up their wrists.
Matching dangly hearts!

I slip mine on
wrap my arms around her and
shake my head fiercely.

I don't even want to go.

Then let me go for you, says Cristina,
and my friends since forever
laugh
even though I know
Cristina's a little jealous
(she told me so).

I try not to cry but Rosamie,
well, she's a waterfall.

I change the subject
to Mark Santos
our group crush
and we're
eating and
talking and
laughing again

      just like normal.

Lunch is almost done so
I run to the bathroom
but when I return
I see they're
eating and
talking and
laughing again

      just like normal.

As if I'm already gone.

WITHOUT MAMA

I used to wonder
when we'd reunite again.
Finally, it's time.

FIVE YEARS AGO

When I was seven, life was good but hard.

Good meant
playing with friends through the countryside
eating green mango soaked in vinegar and salt
while watching Lolo prune trees
the mountains behind him
climbing up to the sky.

Hard meant
Lola cutting the tips of my shoes
to make room for my growing feet
Mama working many jobs
because sometimes Lolo got sick
needing medicine and care.

Good but hard
because even though
my toes poked through
at the end of the day
when the sun sank
and shone its low light,
I'd stroll with Mama and Lola
down pathways
and we'd
walk and talk and watch
as the
sun
      went
           down.

Hard but good because
even though I wished
for new dresses and books
or to do fun things
instead of my own job
washing laundry for extra pesos,
I had my friends.
I had my school that I loved.
I had a mother who said
One day, Isabel,
things will be different.

You can dream and do.

She always told me that.
I can dream and do, too
she said.
I'm going to help us.
I have a plan.

      A sacrifice.

That's the word
I heard it called.
I didn't know what she meant
or how her plan would
change
my
path.

HOW IT STARTED

Mama left because of brochures

> *Looking for Overseas Filipino Workers.*

Brochures for

> cruise ship maids
> cruise ship cooks
> hotel maids
> hotel cooks
> nurses in hospitals
> nurses in care homes
> nannies for families.

In places like

> Hong Kong
> Saudi Arabia
> Japan
> England
> Australia
> America.

The cruise ship brochure had

> bedrooms for princesses
> blond kids with big smiles
> slipping down water slides
> and happy, silent servers
> working mile-long tables
> topped with towering cakes.

In every brochure

    the workers looked like Mama
    the kids looked nothing like me.

ONE
NIGHT

while
my
family
slept
I snuck
looks
and
flipped
pages,
wondering
about
those
kids
their
lives,
imagining
how
it
felt
to
rush
down
a
cool
water
s l i d e.

SACRIFICE

An agency called

Mama got the job!

A one-year contract
as a nanny for a family
in New York
to three children
around my age
Nicolette, Fiona, and Hunter.
I'd never heard names like that.

Lola said
This is hard work, anak.
Maybe you can find hard work
in your own country.
Maybe in Manila.
The city has
more opportunities.

But Mama said a small salary
through a good agency
meant
double or triple the pesos
over any job in Manila.

It meant
medicine for Lolo
new shoes for me
and that Lolo and Lola didn't have
to work so hard.

Maybe I can finish nursing school
—and college one day for Isabel, too.
Working an ocean away means more.

Lola knew people from our town
who had left, but she said
she wished
it was easier
in her country
for people to

        stay.

WHEN MAMA SAID GOODBYE

A five-hour drive
from our province to the city
Mama up front with an uncle
me wedged in back
between Lola and Auntie Flor.
Flor would help with Mama away.

At the airport
kids my age and younger
sold trinkets and gum
garlands like ours
begging

Do you want to buy?

looking
so tattered and skinny
so worse off than me
not to have a mother
with an opportunity.

At the gate
Mama shared her plan.
She'd call every Saturday
she'd try it out temporarily.

Lola cried.
I tried to focus only on Mama.

Her kiss on my forehead
her hands on mine
her eyes saying goodbye.

GOODBYE, GARDEN

My last meal at home.
Lola fixes dinner and asks

Can you grab some calamansi, Isa?

I run to the garden
to our bountiful tree.

> Family legend has it that
> growing this garden helped Lolo
> after his return from World War II,
> where he fought alongside
> Filipinos and Filipino Americans,
> that this garden restored
> his mind and soul
> that growing vegetables
> helped my grandparents get their
> market business started.

> After Mama left
> whenever I missed her
> he'd take me
> here
> his sacred place.
> I'd close my eyes
> and listen
> to morning songs of
> deep croaking frogs
> the wind whistling through trees

his calm, low voice describing
what had grown in the night.

Kamote, talong, sitaw.

Sweet potatoes, eggplant, green beans.

I love this garden.
I love my hands dug into rich soil
when Lolo tries to teach me
the importance of growing
even though my thumb's not green.

I love this garden
for the bounty it brings
but what I can't forget here are

Mama's goodbyes.

I've only seen my mother
five times in five years.
Whenever she visits

she acts surprised
that I've grown.
She sobs
takes my hand through
a thousand shades of green,
reveling in the
height of the calamansi tree
planted when I was a baby,
making me reach up my arms
for a quick photo to show

how I've grown
against its limbs
since the last one she took.

Yesterday in a tourist book
Lolo showed me pictures
of my new city
with a Golden Gate Bridge
and a Golden Gate Park.

Look, there's a huge garden in that park!
he said. His eyes lit up.
Mine did not.

Isabel! Calamansi, please!
Lola calls.

I pluck a ripe greenish one
not to sell at the market
but for my favorite meal.
I offer to cook instead of Lola
but she smiles and says
Let's cook together.

So we do
and we dance
in between
chopping and mixing
simmering and smelling
holding on and letting go.

SPREAD

DINNER ADVICE

LOLO
Please call
Eat all your vegetables
Make good friends

LOLA
Once a week
Say all your prayers
Get good grades

Enjoy California!

ME
But what if I miss home?

Easy.
When things feel hard
find the familiar.
The people
places
things
that feel like
home.

But how?

You'll know when you see them.

We promise.

NOW IT'S MY TURN

Mama wanted to come home
to fly with me to California
but it was too expensive.
She thought I could handle
a solo flight adventure.
I thought so, too,
but as we reach the airport
I'm not so sure.

The plan

She'll meet me in San Francisco.
We'll stay with her cousin,
my Auntie Grace,
until we find
our own place to live.

I'll go to sixth grade

I'll do well in school

I'll meet new friends

I'll make everyone proud.

NOW BOARDING

Lola, Auntie Flor, and I
find my gate and
Auntie hands me
a stack of magazines
Sassy, YM
Seventeen, Teen Beat

You can read these on the ride, Isa
she says with a smile
I try to return
but how
when I'm about to fly
over
six thousand
nine hundred
miles from Manila
to San Francisco

all on my own?

DREAM VACATION

On the plane
passengers file past.

I open and close the tray
turn the air valve to *whoosh!*
push the lever that moves my seat
forward and back.

       When do we take off?

I'd always thought
my first plane ride would be
to visit Mama in New York.

She used to describe
the crowds and playgrounds
the tall buildings lit up at night.
I wanted to visit so badly.

Soon, anak, she'd say
—but I never did.

Except really
if I think about it
I only wanted to go
to meet the family
who took her away

those new people
she called home.

UP IN THE AIR

Twelve hours up here
is a whole lot of boring
but the airplane has
free animated movies
peanuts in a tinfoil bag
a perky flight attendant
who checks up on me
and a nice Filipina auntie
who gave me the window seat
when she learned
I was traveling alone.

She pats my hand.

I'm Tita Rosa.
I will stay with you, anak,
when we get off the plane
until your family arrives.

I shift and shift
in this stiff, upright seat
then open a magazine
straight to a quiz.

Oh, my daughters loved
those quizzes!
says the flight attendant
wheeling a cart.
Here.

She hands me
a stubby pencil
and I get to work.

DESIGN YOUR OWN BEDROOM!

Choose:

Your favorite color combo

Pink and green

A pattern

Butterflies

Your dream vacation

New York

An animal

A bumblebee

A texture

The mountains

A favorite pastime

Cooking and baking

Points scored: 12

Your result?

Colorful Kid!

You're eclectic and sunny
you love new things
you live for adventure.
Try a garden motif
or flower patterns
to show off your whimsical style!

AN OVERNIGHT FLIGHT

As the sun leaves the sky
the pilot announces
in Tagalog before English
the cabin lights dimming
a smooth flight over oceans.
When you wake you'll be
in San Francisco.
His voice is deep and buttery
maybe like a father's
though I wouldn't know
since Lolo's the only dad
I've ever had.

I raise the shade
and peek out
above clouds
above water
into an endless darkening night
trying so hard to picture
my brand-new life.

YESTERDAY

Dusk
through our town
miles and mountains
Manila streets
shanties lining the roads
nighttime lights
snaking cars
everything so crowded
it blurred.

TODAY

Daybreak
through the airport
cars and parking lots
San Francisco hills
skinny houses on steep streets
morning towers
dinging trolleys
everything so crowded
it blurs.

WE'RE LANDING

A faceless voice announces
We're in for a smooth landing.
Welcome to San Francisco
where the local time is five a.m.

The tita next to me
makes the sign of the cross.

The plane
bumps as we land.

Everyone on board
claps like it's a show.

NO MORE GOODBYES

The flight attendant
leads me out
bodies and faces
my wobbly legs
my trembly heart
scanning for her.

BUT MAMA'S NOT HERE

It's Auntie Grace and Uncle Angelo
greeting me through the whir.
Auntie puts her arms around me
and kisses both cheeks.

Oh, Isabel, anak! You made it!
How was your flight?

Her words sound jumbled
but I know it's my brain.

    Where's Mama?

Oh, your mom will be at the house soon.
Job-hunting stuff. I told her not to worry,
that we'd come get you.
A lot of changes for you both, huh!

Uncle hugs me, too.
Let's find your bags, my dear
and we're moving

        through lines

     through crowds

        nerves pounding

    mind racing

       until finally

we reach
a quiet car

the doors closed
a freeway on-ramp
my head on the window
as the sun comes up.

WHERE AM I?

Auntie turns and grins.
We have a bit of a drive
but you'll get a little
tour of the city!

What I see matches
the pictures from Lolo's book.

Sloping streets
a sparkly bay
grids of wires up high.

A red cable car rolls by
with no passengers yet
not like jeepneys back home
covered in trinkets and people.

No green
         just cement.

No mountains
         just buildings.

My grandparents said
look for familiar things
but there's
nothing here
I recognize.

WHERE ARE WE?

Down more blocks
past more buildings
into neighborhoods now.

This area is called Bernal Heights
says Uncle. *It's where
many Filipinos settled in
the sixties, seventies, eighties
into today*

Nineteen Ninety-Nine.

He turns the wheel
a sharp right.

Hang on tight!

I look up and up and up.
The street is on
the sharpest incline,
a different kind of mountain
                                I'm
                        scared
                    the car
                might
            slip
backwards!

Yikes!

Oh, you'll get used to it
laughs Auntie
and soon we've reached
streets of skinny houses
so close to each other
that I can't imagine
space for gardens.

Home, sweet home
says Uncle.

MAYBE SHE'S INSIDE?

We walk up some steps
into a clean house with
cream carpets and
healthy plants
potted in corners.

> I glance around.
> Mama's not here.

Welcome, Isabel, says Auntie

> as I stand there
> not knowing what
> to say or do.

I made some rice!
Let's eat breakfast,
you'll feel much better.

Auntie gives me a side hug.
For a moment I shut my eyes
and pretend she's Lola
instead of a stranger
in a new country.

OTHER KIDS

The room where I'll sleep
with Mama has two beds
belonging to my twin cousins,
Belinda and Blessica,
posters hung all over
fairy lights strung like stars
and paper butterflies
dangling from the ceiling.

This room as a quiz result would be

     Totally Trendy.

The twins are away at college
in a place where it snows.
Mama used to describe snow
as surprising, a white blanket.
She showed me pictures
of those kids she nannied
sledding
and I wondered
if it seemed as fun
as it looked.

On the nightstand I see
the twins' framed photo,
their confident, sparkly smiles.

We've only met once
me at seven, them thirteen.

I remember how they reacted
visiting my home for the first time.
They laughed at the roosters
who crowed them awake
hated all the summertime bugs
begged their parents to go to Manila
for a shopping day.

We threw their family
a welcome party.
Everyone in town came
and the twins asked
jokingly, but sort of real

How can we be related to all these people?

As I sit at their dresser
a short-term intruder
their surprise there
was maybe like
my surprise here.

WHAT LOLA PACKED

All my belongings fit into
three empty drawers

clothes
magazines
stuff Lola packed that
I didn't know about until now

pictures with my friends
pictures with my grandparents
and something else

a bamboo box with

Lolo's favorite gardening gloves
unopened packets of seeds
(that Mama had sent me once)
my favorite candy
in bright wrappers
like I was
seven or something.
I unwrap one.
Sweetness seeps
onto my tongue.

Finally
a tiny glass bottle
the height of my pinky.
Without opening it
I know it holds
a calming, soothing scent

Jasmine
     Sampaguita

Lola's magic trick
for whenever I feel bad.

I put the pictures on the dresser.
One photo's already there
me onstage getting top honors
my neck draped with flowers
my grandparents snapped it
since Mama couldn't come.

HAMBURGER CALL

On the nightstand sits a phone
shaped like a hamburger
the top a plastic bun
with plastic lettuce and tomatoes
and a long spiraled cord.

The phone rings.
The door opens.

Isabel, it's your grandparents!
Auntie points to the phone.
I flip it open.

   Hello?

Their voices
sixteen hours ahead
settling
soothing
and though they seem
happy, I can tell by
Lola's soft shaky words
this will be as
different for me as
for them, too.

THERE

After Mama left us
she called every week
with the same questions

How's everything?

But what was there to say?

That I missed her
but hated her?
That worries
clouded my head
like how I thought she'd
stay
with that family
forever?

You're turning twelve soon,
my Isabel.
Twelve!
And I'm so proud of
your top honors!
Lola sent me the picture!

I could hear her
waiting breath.

But what was there to say?

That I loved her
but hated her?

That turning twelve meant
I had so many questions
but didn't know who to ask?

It was Lolo who'd
walk me through the garden
saying
Time to be strong, anak

but it was me who decided
how
so the next time Mama asked

How's everything?

I learned to say
without hesitation

> *Fine, Mama, just fine.*

And that's what I told her
each time

> *Fine. Everything's fine.*

THERE TO HERE

Why hasn't Mama come yet?
Like waiting for sprouts to bloom.
Five years down to here and now.
Finally, the door opens.

NOW

She runs over
reaches fast
grabs me so tight
then stands back.

Oh, my Isabel!
We're as tall as each other now!
She begins to cry.
I can't believe it. We're here now

    together now.

I've tried so many times
to remember her scent
warm and clean
eventually forgetting
so much about her
but not any longer
because she's here now

    together now

my anger melting as she
draws me near again
holds me close again
as I tighten my grip

    and I'm never letting go.

SAMPAGUITA

The Philippines' national flower.

Glossy green leaves
five white whorls
small and dainty
star-shaped blossoms.

Jasminum sambac
its species

Jasmine
its common name

A flower
cultivated everywhere
especially Asia.
Some bloom at night
some bloom year-round
but no matter the type
it's a reminder of
home.

PROMISES

Lola grew and sold sampaguita.

As garlands hung from her wrists
walking through open-air markets
shouting:

Necklaces! Necklaces!

As oil turned into candles
to purify homes and keep evil away.

As full blooms to Chinese neighbors
who brewed it for tea.

As a way to pretty up hair
or spice up lotion
or calming me with its scent
whenever I felt sad.

Until Mama started
sending her boxes,
the flower gave my family
pesos and promises.
Lola told me their history once
that it wasn't native, but
brought by 17th-century travelers
until it grew into the landscape and

stayed.

MEETING MORE FAMILY

My first day in California
ends in the backyard.
It's not a Lolo garden.

> Still pretty though
> I don't recognize the plants.

There's one other family here
distant relatives
a distant cousin.

> Still family though
> we've never met.

There's a table of dishes
like in any Filipino house (rich or poor).
Italian, takeout, new to me.

> Still tasty even though
> I crave Filipino food.

Lolo said when things feel hard
look for the familiar
but what happens if
the things I see
are right and wrong
distant and familiar?

MEETING A NEW COUSIN

Jocelyn is in tenth grade.
Joss for short, she says.
Her smile comes quick,
the nice kind.
Are you nervous for school?

Mama beams at me.
Isa starts next week.
But first, some
back-to-school shopping.

I went to Bayview Middle.
Joss scans me.
Just pick a good outfit
for your first day.
You know,
to blend in.

       I wasn't nervous until now.

Joss looks like one of those girls
from one of those magazines
stylish and pretty,
oozing with confidence.
If she's a California kid
I'll look
nothing
like anyone
at school.

ONE DAY WE'LL GROW IT HERE

Miles away
I'm feeling it now
heavy on my eyes
I'm hearing it now
everyone's voices blending.

Lolo said I'd feel jet-lagged.
If this was dinner
in his garden
the scent of jasmine
would waft over
waking me
soothing me
but no trace here
as I inhale.

Mama rubs my back.

When we have our own yard
we'll grow a garden like Lolo's.
We can start with jasmine.
Somehow she's read my mind.

> *Would that grow here?*

I don't see why not.

I'm thinking of my

Jasmine
      Sampaguita

back home in the garden
sad and unsettled.
I wish I'd given it
a better start.

When Mama and I
have our own yard
I'll grow another.

It's the only way
I'll ever
see
my home
here.

ROOT

BA·LIK·BAY·AN

noun Philippines

1. a Filipino visiting or returning to live in the Philippines after living in another country.

BA·LIK·BAY·AN BOX

noun Philippines

1. a carton shipped to friends and relatives in the Philippines by a Filipino who has been living overseas, typically containing items such as food, clothing, toys, and household products.

HER FIRST VISIT HOME

After Mama left
her first visit home was
by balikbayan box.
That's how I saw her
once a month—
a huge brown box
with presents inside
for everyone.

Little things
like

> vitamins
> aspirin
> medicine
> clothes
> candles
> corned beef
> canned Spam
> shampoo
> conditioner
> pretty pink lipsticks for the aunties

Big things
like

> an espresso machine for Lola
> a silver watch for Lolo

And things just for me
like

        books, toys
        socks, tees
        brand-new shoes
        gardening gloves
        seed packets
        and once, during Christmas,
        a snow globe of
        New York in winter
        with fake flakes
        that swirled when I shook it.

Each month I waited
for her box
as if it was
a real
live
visit.

ALL THE THINGS SHE MISSED

The few times
Mama came home for real,
two weeks in summer,
never felt like enough.
I wanted to see her during
all the things she missed
like birthdays
Saturdays
spring days
planting days
my first period
my first crush
and all the days in between.

ENVELOPE

Mama's boxes always had

envelopes

with Lola or Lolo's name,
and always with money.
Once
there came an

envelope

for me.

To My Isabel

I tore it open.

Inside
a twenty-dollar bill
worth much more in pesos,
and a note for Auntie Flor
in Mama's swirly writing:

Please take Isabel and Lola
to that big mall in Manila
for Isa's eighth birthday!

BIRTHDAY GIFT

I'd heard of it.
A giant mall with
four stories and
escalators reaching
to the tallest ceiling.

Oh, wow.

Auntie, Lola, and I
spent the day wandering,
mainly looking
a bit of buying.

After lunch at Jollibee
of burgers and spaghetti
(so tasty!)
I spotted a bookstore
with cookbooks and
found my own
mini culinary school
in one hundred brightly colored pages.

Every picture popped
so bright and pretty
so mouthwatering
an invitation
for my new hobby.

MY FAVORITE MEMORY

It's neat how even
a book can feel
like an old friend.

I dog-eared that cookbook
wrote in it like a diary
why I cooked something
where I cooked it
like my first cake
for Lola's birthday.

I'd held
a bag of flour
and Lolo scared me
on purpose.
He thought it'd be funny
but I startled
and it rained
a puffy cloud
settling softly.
So much laughter
as we cleaned up.

Me and the only father
I'd ever known.

FIRST MORNING HERE

I wake up through the jet lag.
Paper cutout butterflies
dangle down from the ceiling.
Feels like a dream, but it's not.

BREAKFAST HERE

is garlic rice and eggs,
sweet longanisa.
Tastily familiar.

Finally.

At the kitchen table Uncle Angelo
reads a newspaper and gives it a snap.

Look, it's you
he says to Auntie Grace,
beaming and pointing.

They got my bad side
she says, jokingly.

They look at the paper together
and he gives her a little shoulder rub.
They love each other, I can tell.
Something I never saw growing up
was a dad and a mom together.
Mama never talked about my father
so I never asked.

*Your auntie's working hard
for our community, Isabel.*

He shows me the headline:

"Asian American Senior Center Trying to Raise Funding"

That's where I'm a nurse
Auntie says.
It's a good organization but
those seniors need so much more
than what they currently have.

Mama hurries in
grabs her purse.

Wish me luck, Isa.
Another interview!

Mama took nursing classes in New York
now she's looking for hospital jobs.
School in the day
work in the night
My mother sacrifices
wherever she lives.

She pulls out an envelope
hands it to Auntie and grins.

Have fun, you two.
Your auntie's a master shopper.

I am!
Auntie winks at me.
I miss shopping with the twins, you know.
We'll make up for that today.

I'd hoped
Mama and I
would have

today

but no

she's off to settle
our brand-new life
and I'm out the door
for some brand-new outfits.

MY NEW SCHOOL

Auntie and I stroll,
the sun on our faces
the air chilly
even in summer.
We pass
trees planted in cement
and every street
climbs and falls
dips and drops.

I may never get used to this.

Your manangs Belinda and Blessica
knew this neighborhood
inside and out
so will you
says Auntie.
Your lola tells me you're
very independent!
It's good to explore.

More blocks down
she pauses and points.
There's where I work.
Let's stop in.

THE SENIOR CENTER

A tall brick building
nothing fancy,
windows, a lobby
big swaths of sunlight.

Nurses and seniors
clipboards and wheelchairs
like pages from a brochure.

The first people
Auntie spots are
a man and a girl,
both Filipino.

Eric! says Auntie.

He waves, walks over.

You must be Isabel
says the man, a big smile.
*I'm Eric Mabalon,
the activities director here.
This is my daughter, Missy.
You'll both be at
the same school soon.*

He smiles. The girl doesn't.

Let's go now, Dad.

*Actually, kiddos, I could use
your quick help, please.*

Is that okay? he asks Auntie,
and she nods.

Suddenly we're swarmed
by friendly older women,
Lola types,
mainly Filipino-looking
and other older Asian people, too.
Nice smiles. Kind words.

Melissa!
Nice to see you!
Who's your friend?

Before the girl can respond
Eric points to some boxes.
Girls, would you mind helping me
bring these to the patio?

One older woman giggles.
He called us girls, girls
and Melissa and I laugh, too.
I'm Lola Yoling, she says to me.
Come, I'll take you.

SEEING HOME

Lola Yoling leads us through
the rec room
the dining room,
pausing every few paces
to introduce me to
more lolos and lolas
who look like
they could be related,
reminding me of
my grandparents with
their dark eyes like mine,
their same wide noses.
In their faces
I see my old home.
I feel the comfort
of something familiar.

ON THE PATIO

Eric opens a box, holds up
small reddish pots
that the old women admire.

Some fun donations, he says.
Soil's coming tomorrow
some plants, too.
We'll have fun, ladies!

Oh, wonderful!
Lola Yoling clasps her hands.
We could use some green back here.

An older man joins us,
Lola Yoling's husband,
—Lolo Frank.
I was taught to call
every elder Lolo or Lola
out of respect.

Lolo Frank scans the supplies.
Whatever happened to
the gardening program?
That outdoor time was
good for my muscles.

You have muscles?
Lola Yoling chuckles
and says to me and Melissa
We used to garden with
the school down the street.

Bayview Middle?
says Melissa.
That's my school this year.

Other residents chime in
with school garden memories.

*I heard the garden's
not in use anymore*
says Lolo Frank.
Too bad.

Melissa, Isabel
says Lola Yoling,
*you remind me of my daughters
when they were your age.*

Melissa smiles.
Where are they now?

*Far away.
I wish I saw them more.*

We wind back to the lobby
and I notice
the rec room is worn
frayed couches
stained rugs
and I remember
what Uncle Angelo read
how this place needs funding.

Promise you'll come back?
says Lola Yoling.

The girl and I both nod.

Melissa glances at me.
Suddenly
I'm pinged with sadness
thinking of Cristina and Rosamie.

Auntie says
*Girls, I hope you'll
see each other at school*
and Melissa and I nod
as my aunt leads me out.

ALL ARE WELCOME

Stepping into sunshine
a few more blocks.
Auntie points.

There it is, your new school!

We inch closer
I peer through the gate.
Courtyards and quads
Rows of metal lockers.

We walk the perimeter.
Around back I spot
a weathered sign
a separate area:

School Garden. All Are Welcome.

That must be what
the seniors talked about.

I try to picture myself
here
without my friends.
A pretzel knots
in my stomach.

We keep walking
and reach a busy area
of people and shops.

BACK-TO-SCHOOL SHOPPING

I kept the magazines
from the plane.
One of the ads with girls my age
wearing overalls, chunky-soled shoes,
confident, sparkly smiles.

What do kids wear on
their first days of school
in their brand-new life?

PEOPLE ALL AROUND

At Union Square
there's a cavernous store
multiple stories tall called Macy's,
with really good sales, says Auntie.
The escalator takes us up and up
into the section of
those clothes from
those magazines.

Unlike the senior center
Not everyone looks
like what I know.
There's black hair, brown hair, blond
every shade of skin.
Lolo had said in America
I'd see a melting pot.

We weave through
colors fabrics styles
that don't
seem like me or
look like me
—but then again
what does?

I spot denim overalls.

Cute!

Auntie scans the tag.

Sorry, anak, too expensive.
Let's
use your mama's money
wisely.

ANOTHER GIRL

I notice a girl
maybe my age
light-haired, light-skinned.
She eyes me.
I half smile but
she doesn't.

She can probably tell
how out of place I feel
how out of place I've felt
since I stepped off that plane

      like I don't belong here.

For a moment
in my head I pretend
I'm someone different.
A California girl shopping
with her California mom
just like this girl
looking at the same overalls,
except her mom's holding them up
saying, *Try them on!*

I pick out a few nice things
and Auntie says
I have good feelings
about your first day
on Monday.

Monday?
Today's Friday.

There's that pretzel again
twisting as tight
as it will go.

A SWIRL

Auntie ends our day
with one more stop.
I think you'll like this.

We ride a cable car
rolling the street
watching tourists like me
ending near a busy spot
Pier 39
where sea lions bark
and things smell fishy.

No sampaguita sold here.

We stroll
through crowds and
stop at a souvenir store.

Pick something! From me.
To remember your first
San Francisco outing
with your auntie.
She beams.

The keychain kiosk
doesn't have my name
so instead I choose
a snow globe
with no snow
only a bridge

that looks more red
than golden.
When I shake it
a swirling storm
of glitter
not knowing
how to land.
Eventually
it clears.

STILL TRYING TO SPOT ANYTHING FAMILIAR

We end with lunch
a view of the bay
clam chowder in bread bowls.

I see three girls
my age
racing through the bustle
and I remember
me, Cristina, and Rosamie
on market days
having the same kind of fun.
An empty thud in my chest.
Who do I run with now?

I think of Lolo's advice
trying to keep spotting
the familiar.

Our clam chowder comes
and that first cozy bite
oh my yum.

Except
it's followed by
the feeling that
I wish my grandparents
could taste this,
too.

THINGS ABOUT HER I DON'T KNOW

That night Mama, Auntie, and I
drive to a party in Daly City
thrown in our honor by
lolos and lolas, titos and titas
who immigrated here
long before I was born.

In the car Mama and her cousin gab.
Turns out Mama's visited San Francisco
before—I never knew that.
California was closer than the Philippines.

I listen as Mama talks
and realize
her accent
is there, but faded.
She sounds more like Auntie
who's lived in the United States
longer than I've been alive.

Did she mean for that to happen?

MY AMERICAN FAMILY

We reach a house
full of people
full of food.
There's even a cake:

Welcome to California!

Different lolas rush up
like one tiny woman who takes
my face in her hands
this grandma I've never seen,
with puckered skin
as if she sat in water for days.

Oh, Isabel, anak! You're here! At last!

They all know my story.

The house thumps
it's so loud
like parties at home.

She shoves me
an empty plate
and says
Go eat! Go eat!
Definitely something I know.

I pile my plate
follow TV sounds
into a room with

cousins on couches.
Joss waves me over.

I sneak glances
through the thickness of
my American family
doing the same things
like parties at home

eating
gossiping
laughing

all of it
familiar and not.

MEET THE COUSINS

Jocelyn's in ninth grade
Older than her brother, Junior, and cousin, Tessa
Casually chic
English is her only language
Loves to give advice
Yaks in a good way
Nice, not nerdy

Junior is Jocelyn's younger brother
Unafraid of his big sister
Nintendo keeps him busy
Instant bully (in a cousin kind of way)
Obnoxious
Really, really obnoxious

Tessa's also in high school and seems
Easygoing
Sweet
Smiley
Another distant cousin, another possible friend

THE COUSINS' ADVICE

Sooooo
what did you end up buying? asks Joss.
Nothing nerdy,
I hope
but she says this like she's joking.

Quietly
I tell her
> *jeans*
> *some skirts and shirts,*
> *a dress with cute sunflowers.*
> *Nothing too nerdy,*
> *I hope.*

Don't worry about that stuff
says Tessa
in her
cute tank top + butterfly clips + flared pants.
You'll be fine.

Junior chimes in, mouth full
hands glued to the controllers.
Just don't talk out loud,
you know, like when you're
in public at school
so they can't hear you're like all
Fresh Off the Boat
Hahahahahahaha!

His sister and cousin whack him.

Dude
Shut up
*What if you were sent to the Philippines to live there and you'd
never been there before and you had a Valley girl accent. Huh?
HUH?*

Tessa says
*Junior would never last there he'd get eaten by mosquitoes or
starve to death because he hates anything that's not Chicken
McNuggets or Flamin' Hot Cheetos and doesn't even know how to
microwave his own Cup O' Noodles!*

We all laugh at that one
(except him)
but now
one more worry
pops up in fury.

Because if *they* notice how different I sound
these strangers who look like *me*
come from the same place as *me*
are somehow blood-related

then what will

strangers at school

think?

A WEIRD PHONE CALL

We're back at Auntie and Uncle's
at the end of a long day and night.

The phone rings.
Auntie answers,
an eyebrow raised:
It's for you, Cora.

After Mama's *Hello?*
I hear:
Hi, Nicolette, sweetheart.
It's so late your time. Everything all right?

That name.
It's the oldest girl, sixteen,
of the family she nannied.
Mama's described her before as
really smart and really sweet.
I don't know how she's
described me.

Auntie and Uncle talk at the table
and it's hard to hear Mama's words
—or the girl's.

I get up and pretend
I'm going to the bathroom
but instead slip quietly
into the bedroom and
reach for a hamburger.

WHAT I HEAR

Carefully
stealthily
quietly
I lift the bun.

I wish you were here, Cora,
instead of Mom.
She's so not fair.
She won't let me go to the dance!
I miss you, Cora.
Please come back?
I hate our new nanny.
She doesn't even know
how to do anything.

Listen to your mother, dear.
She has rules, and she loves you.

You're more my mom
than she will ever be.
It's so different
now that you're gone.
I wish you'd come home.
I miss you. We all do.

I miss you, too, dear.

Home.

That's what the girl called it.
Mama didn't disagree.

Carefully
stealthily
quietly
I put the bun back down.

MORE THINGS ABOUT HER I DIDN'T KNOW

Why would that girl call
asking Mama to come home?
My mom's the stranger.

FIRST DAY

In the Philippines
students wear uniforms.
Mine was
a white buttoned-up shirt,
a knee-length red skirt
the same deep hue
of a sweet spiky rambutan
fallen on the road,
that the boys would throw
at me and my friends
as we walked home
arm in arm
ducking and laughing
since the boys always missed.

No uniforms here at
Bayview Middle School.

I wear
a new outfit and
slightly terrified eyes.

WHILE ENTERING

a swarming courtyard,
kids collide
like a
pinball machine
gone bananas.

I DON'T BELONG HERE

Some kids look like me,
brown skin, black hair,
Filipino or Asian,
but others look only like
the girls in those magazines
light hair, light skin
shiny smiles.

My heart thumps so fast.
One kid glances my way
and I wonder
if it's because
my heart's beating so loud
that he can hear
how nervous I feel.

MORE PINBALL

Ears

                    ringing
          head

                              racing
                    eyes
          searching

                    courtyard

          clearing

everyone

          running

but

          I

                    can't

          find

my

          class!

PHEW

That's when I spot it.
I rush inside the classroom.
I'm the last one in.

WELCOME TO HOMEROOM

Welcome to English Homeroom
I'm Mrs. Kapoor
she says with a kind smile
that lowers my nerves
from high to medium-high.

I'm going to have you all
introduce yourselves
she says
and my nerves
crank back up.
But first a little more about
me and my class.
Been teaching thirty years.
My grown children are proud
Bayview Bolts.
Here you'll learn
writing, books, poetry . . .
skills for life.

Like how to burp your ABCs?
says the voice behind me.
Everyone snickers.

Your name, good sir?

Marcus. Marcus Pangilinan.

   He looks Filipino like me.

Marcus, since you're
so willing to jump in
I'll have you begin.
We'll work our way around.
Please come up to the front.

For a second her eyes meet mine.
Great. She'll probably
call on me next.

SHARE TWO THINGS

1. What you did over the summer.

2. What you're looking forward to this fall.

WHAT THE OTHER KIDS DID

Marcus swaggers
front and center
the kind of kid
who would've thrown a rambutan
at me and my friends.

For the summer
Marcus went to Disneyland.
For the fall
Marcus wants to win the talent show
by shining miniature flashlights
on and off into each of his nostrils
in a darkened auditorium
to the tune of
"Livin' La Vida Loca."

Everyone loves Marcus's intro.
They even clap.

Shoot. What interesting thing
do I say?

Luckily, Mrs. Kapoor points
to the student near Marcus.

Brandi. Really pretty.
Deep dark skin.
A clear loud voice.

I moved to a new house
this summer

and I want to make Pep Squad
this fall.

My heartbeat races.
My head buzzes.
On go these intros
up and down rows.
Not my turn yet—but almost.
First, the girl I met
at the senior center.

WE LOOK THE SAME BUT NOT

Melissa Mabalon
is someone I can't help
but stare at because
she looks like me
but doesn't.
Black hair, brown skin.
Filipino, too, but in a
different way than me.

Melissa went to Hawaii over
the summer.
This fall
she wants to run for sixth-grade class prez.

Remember to vote for me!
she says all sparkly smiley.
I sneak my eyes right then left
and girls on both sides nod like
they're in a Melissa Fan Club.

Mrs. Kapoor looks at me.

Last but not least.

GULP

My bottom feels glued to the chair.
I walk up, rack my brain as they stare.
So what should I say
in an interesting way?
Or will I just faint in despair?

FINDING MY TALENT

A room of faces staring
reminds me of when I was nine and
Auntie Flor convinced Lola I should
enter a Little Miss Ilocos Sur contest.

For the talent part
I couldn't dance (no rhythm)
couldn't sing (squawk like a chicken)
so I read a poem,
one that Lolo chose
called "Desiderata."

Go placidly amid the noise and the haste
and remember what peace there may be in silence.
As far as possible without surrender,
be on good terms with all persons.
Speak your truth quietly and clearly,
and listen to others,
even the dull and ignorant;
they too have their story.
Be yourself.

I'd practiced and memorized
but at the last minute
changed it in my head
I thought I needed
something snazzier.
Mine went

I want to win
Miss Philippines
so I can ride
a limousine
my favorite cake
has vanilla beans.
Salamat and thank you!!!!!

I added a bow.

Auntie's mouth gaped so wide
flies might shoot in
but I liked what I recited.

The audience clapped
politely
except for Lola who hooted
and Lolo who whistled like he was
hailing a cab in Manila.

In the end I didn't place
(not even close)
but I wouldn't have won
anyway
my skin too dark
even among other Filipinos
my outfits not shiny enough
like the contestants with money,
only clean hand-me-downs
sent from New York,
dresses once belonging to

those kids Mama nannied and
so many shoes
because they had
so many pairs.

BE YOURSELF

Faces from
front to back
watch, wait
ready
to hear about my
Disneyland or Hawaiian adventure.

I could fib.
I could have brought my souvenirs
like my Grand Canyon fanny pack
or my Donald and Goofy sweatshirt
or the Empire State Building keychain
—gifts from Mama
who would visit a new place
each summer
with Nicolette, Hunter, and Fiona
sending pictures in her balikbayan boxes
like that was the same as giving us
our own memories.

Mrs. Kapoor smiles.
Go ahead, dear.

I can tell them how
I rode a plane
ate peanuts
did quizzes.

My hands shake
my body aches
my voice cracks

and my accent slips through.

BE YOURSELF (BUT DON'T MESS UP)

I'm Isabel.
This summer
I moved here
This fall
I want . . .

. . . to make new friends.

Thanks. Thank you.
Ummm . . . yeah.

I race back to my seat
in between Melissa and Marcus
the two kids in class
who look like me.

Marcus says, really loudly,
Ya sound like my lola!
and kids around us crack up.

Melissa turns
her eyes passing mine
meeting his.

He snorts. She shakes her head.

Only kind words in this room, please
says Mrs. Kapoor.

In every class until lunch
through all the other intros
no one else has
an accent like mine
—or even has one at all.

IN THE CLASS BEFORE LUNCH

A handout: *Meet the Teachers*
Parents, It's Back-to-School Night!
Mama's missed so many things . . .
I can't wait for her to come.

LUNCHTIME

I scan for an empty spot.

No balete trees here
—only tables filling up.
Fast.

There's one.

Girls clumped tight
five or six of them
pushed to the side
so one is half empty.
The only invitation
I can find
in this whole courtyard.

       Maybe they're friendly?

I make my move.

Without looking at me
synchronized
they slide over
in clump formation.

I touch the bracelet on my wrist
from Rosamie and Cristina and
feel our three smooth hearts
to remind myself
I had best friends once, too.

NO ONE TOLD ME

I unpack the lunch Mama made
a sandwich and chips
a foil pouch (tropical punch).
Maybe these were things
she'd pack for her nanny family.
Nothing like Lola's baon
—containers of rice with tocino
my favorite sweet sausage
or rice with hot dogs cut up,
my favorites.

I take a bite of turkey sandwich.
It tastes like American lunch
in American school.

In the clump
I realize it's Melissa
scooched so far over
like I smell bad or something.

Next to her
a light-haired girl
who seems familiar
wearing cute overalls.
That's when I remember
the girl at Macy's.

The girl's eyes go
from my face down my legs
then grow round as calamansi.

Don't you shave your legs?!?!?!

Ashley! shouts Brandi. *That's soooo rude!*
but they can't stop giggling.
Even Melissa.

I don't know
what to say
what to do
where else to sit.

Without them seeing
I slide out Lola's
tiny glass bottle
from my backpack.
I'd brought it because even
having it near calms me.
I won't smell it now
but still I feel better
knowing it's close.

I pack up
and run off.

Hey, Isabel,
you forgot something?
shouts Melissa
—grabbing Lola's
promises in a bottle
until Ashley

snatches it away.

THE BOTTLE

She holds it up.
What's in here?

> *That's mine.*

I reach.
She doesn't give it back.

*Melissa said you came
from the Philippines.
Is this some sort of
weird Filipino thing?*
She cackles.

Come on, Ashley, give it back
says Melissa—and Brandi, too,
but the girl opens the bottle.

Ewww!

A few of the other girls
lean in to sniff and laugh.

> *Can I have it now, please?*
> I say
> too quietly.

Gross. I don't want this
and the girl throws it
uncapped
so it spills
all over
the table

my shirt
this smell
my home
my heart
feels tainted.

EVERY VISIT AFTER MAMA LEFT

I would sit in the garden
Lola stringing up jasmine.
She'd bring a bloom to my nose,
the scent would settle my heart.

A THING I RECOGNIZE

Not sure where to go now
but I grab the bottle, my backpack,
and walk to the back of the school
until I'm met with a sign:

School Garden. All Are Welcome.

The gate's
broken
but open.
Inside
a garden
but dry.
Browns and yellows.
Weeds not blooms.
A garden to make Lolo
shake his head.

Still, it's empty and
any garden feels like
an old friend.

That's when
something
catches my eye.
A shrub of

Jasmine?
         Sampaguita?

WHY DO I SMELL IT?

A small bush in a large pot.
I'd recognize it anywhere.
But it's brittle and barren
no lush leaves or soft blooms.

       Then why do I smell it?

Oh yeah
my shirt.

There's no sweet scent here
nothing familiar
in this moment.
Not those kids
not cement city
not even Melissa
walking by suddenly
peering in
catching my eye.

She pauses
maybe to make fun
but breaks her gaze
turns and runs
back toward the laughter.

FRIENDSHIP IS A MILLION LITTLE THINGS I MISS

Lunchtime under the balete tree.

Getting googly-eyed over Mark Santos.

After-school snacks and sodas at Rosamie's family's sari-sari store.

A worn-out CD of the Backstreet Boys on repeat.

Inside jokes and juicy talk.

Squeezy surprise hugs whenever days go right . . . or wrong.

Dreams said aloud.

Words spoken without embarrassment.

ANOTHER REMINDER OF HOME

Why did Mama make me move here?

Ten more minutes
until lunch ends.
I'll wait it out
tucked away
no eyes on me
only this bland sandwich
to finish.

In the corner is a bin
with a dusty sign:

> *Can You Dig It?*
> *(Please pack up when finished!)*

Hmmm.

Curiosity strikes.

Inside the bin
are things I know
shears, shovels, forks, gloves
palm-sized packets of seeds.

I take another bite of turkey and wheat
put my sandwich down
and follow my gut
with the shears.
A few snips
a light haircut

so the jasmine's crispy leaves
flutter down
down.

I eat and snip
automatic
imagining I'm home
taking care of
the jasmine with Lolo
forgetting
where I am
for a moment.

SPROUT

WHAT I'LL DO

I
think
of my
jasmine
back home
then look at the
jasmine **here.** A sign.
My second chance to get it
right—and **my only chance**
to ever see home again. I don't have
the best or greenest thumb, but **I**
know this shrub likes water, good
soil, sun or partial shade. Easy things.
I could spend my lunches here.
Bring this empty garden back
to life **one sprout at a time**
so I'll have the
reminder Lolo
told me to
look
for
when
things
get
hard.
I'll **bring my home here** and no one has to know.

MAMA HAD A GARDEN, TOO

Whenever Mama sent pictures
it's how I saw
the kids she nannied,
Nicolette, Hunter, and Fiona,
in their beautiful home
their beautiful backyard where
they played in summers,
with all the sprinklers on.

It's how I knew
how Mama lived.
It's how I knew the family
had a manicured garden
an ivy trellis
a rosebush fence.
That those kids used
little metal spades.
That their hands were
the same size as mine
in bright turquoise gloves
tilling soil
tipping water
holding worms
planting seeds
learning
all the things
she couldn't teach me.

SEEDS IN BOXES

One of Mama's
balikbayan boxes
had all the usual things
little gifts for
every person
but also gardening things like
turquoise gloves, clean and washed
spades from her pictures with those kids
used but shined up like new
unopened packets of seeds
green beans and peas
pumpkins and flowers.

Didn't she know those gloves didn't fit?
That my hands were too grown?
That Lolo already grew green beans?

Didn't she know I never
needed or wanted or wished for
any of those things?
That growing a garden wasn't always fun but
a chore? A way to survive?
That I hated pulling weeds?
That I wanted not to play and not tend?

Didn't she know anything about me?

LOLO USED TO SAY

Did you know that plants are like us?
They have a brain.
They know where they are
and the size they're destined to grow.
They respond to their environment,
like whether it's taken care of or not.
And . . .
They have a voice!
They speak to bees using electrical fields!
To fix a garden look for signs of life
in the roots
check the leaves
find any green
sometimes there's
treasure to resuscitate
with water
good soil
good sun
knowing
there is really
nothing to fix
only to help along
first to survive
then to thrive.

FRIENDS

After the worst first day
I get home with Mama.
The phone rings.
She answers and
waves me over.

A surprise call, Isa!

Lolo on the line says
Girls, she's home!
Hold on, Isabel! Hold on!

We miss you!
Cristina and Rosamie shriek
high-pitched and happy

> *I miss you, too.*
> *What are you doing over there?*

Flores de Mayo.

I'd forgotten.
Each fall
friends visit
to plant and prune flowers
for a festival in May
so by the end of the year
what we planted has bloomed
ready for picking
my favorite yearly tradition.

In the background I hear
the good kind of
group laughter.

How's your new school?

I want to pour out my heart
share this day
—but not ruin theirs.
So, simply I say

  Fine, everything's fine.

ANOTHER CALL

A few minutes later
the phone rings again.
Did they forget
to tell me something?

> *Hello?*

A voice.
A girl's.

That girl.
The oldest one.

Hi.
Is Cora there?
This is Nicolette.

> *This is . . .*
> *Isabel.*

Isabel? she says,
so friendly.
Nice to meet you.
Your mom used to
talk about you
all the time.

> *She . . . did?*

Yeah. You're so lucky.
She's the best.

It's so cool she might be coming
back home to New York.
I just knew I could convince her.

What?

Is she there?
I was calling for advice.
She says it like my mother's
her own mother.

New York?

Isabel?

　　　　No, she's not here.

Can you tell her I called?

I say a quick
yes
then hang up.

Mama comes in

Who was on the phone, anak?

I can't look her in the eye.

　　　　No one. Wrong number.

SOMETHING TO FEEL BETTER

Why did I come
all this way
for Mama to
still talk to those kids?

What did that girl
mean about New York?
Is Mama not sure about
bringing us
together?

*How did you like
your new school?*
My mother smiles.

This call
the bottle
this whole day.

Shouldn't she know me
well enough to guess?
But she doesn't.

    I didn't like it.

What happened, anak?

        *I just . . .
        it's not like my old school.
        Everything's different.*

Uncle comes in and opens the fridge.
A distraction.

I grab my things
and hand her
the Back-to-School flyer.

What's this?

An invitation. For school.

Her face lights up.
This sounds great. I can't wait.
She gives me the best hug.
My heart lightens a little.

AFTER DINNER

Uncle Angelo
calls me over and says

Look, Isa.
You are here.

He unfolds a large map
creased in rectangles.
He points to a blue dot
near the water.
San Francisco.

This is our home.

Some of your mom's side
came to California
in the 1960s and 1970s
and ended up all over.

On this map
of lines and ridges
green for mountains
he points
to more dots

> Stockton
> Lathrop
> Vallejo
> San Bernardino
> Los Angeles.

This map
these places
none of it
I recognize.

He smiles.
I try to return it.

Everything okay, anak?
I heard you in the kitchen.
A tough first day?

      It's fine, Uncle. I'm better now.

It takes time
to know a place.
Maybe it would help you
to know more about
your new home.
I can share some stories
about how
we ended up

here

he says
his finger
meeting a dot.

THERE ARE THOSE WHO CAME BEFORE US

I know you miss your friends
but we are not the first
to leave there for here.
Our home country has
a culture of migration
where leaving means
finding our identities
through our opportunities
elsewhere.

The first Asians
in California
in 1587
were slaves, prisoners
Luzonians, Filipinos
who landed on Morro Bay.

The Pensionados
in 1903
were Filipino scholars
wanting good opportunities
through an act
passed by the US Congress
all of them thinking
education as liberty
though it made for
inequalities.

The Sakadas
in 1906
also called
the First Fifteen.
Filipinos in Hawaii
Manongs
also from Ilocos Sur
like your family
the youngest was
almost your age
—fourteen.
Overseas workers on
sugar plantations
pineapple fields
seeking security
facing discrimination
while sacrificing.

The Alaskeros
in the 1920s
seasonal migrant workers
crew on merchant ships
in fishing canneries
gutting salmon
technically US citizens
from American occupation
treated as worst-class citizens
in cramped cold spaces
traveling west
in off-seasons to labor
on fields and farms.

Many others
fishermen in Louisiana
nurses and teachers imported
nannies, war heroes, war brides
poets turned farmers turned activists
Pinoys, Pinays
unseen, unsung
untold
but we learn from them
how to survive, thrive.
On the Alaskan boats
Filipinos rolled
salmon lumpia.
Salmon lumpia!
Uncle, wide-eyed,
shakes his head.
Can you imagine that?!

So you see, anak
life gets hard
leaving
living in between
here and there
different migrations
different stories
but all spreading roots
making our homes
wherever we are.

UNCLE FOLDS THE MAP BACK UP

He scans my face
and I judge by
his eyes
his voice
his serious tone
that what he's saying
is complicated.

Uncle likes to share.
In the Philippines
he was a high school teacher.
Here
he paints houses
through his painting business
while listening
to history cassettes.

Our people have ties, Isa,
to every dot, every corner
no matter how invisible
we are.
We have spread
our resilience
our unity in strength.
It is quite remarkable, really.
I remember coming here
feeling like
I didn't belong

like nothing made sense.
But the next day
I always tried again.

He pats the paper
a neat, thick rectangle
dots converging in creases
me somewhere
there
but still
like him
not quite sure
where on that map
I belong.

AFTER HOMEWORK

In the bathroom
I find a razor.
Steam swirls and
the water hits my shoulders
like warm Philippine rain.
I shave my legs
nicking twice
knowing that
tomorrow

I'll try again.

MORNING ANNOUNCEMENTS

Every school day begins with the
Bayview Bolts Bulletin.

Marcus volunteers to read
and announces everything
nasally and twangy
until Mrs. Kapoor says
Mr. Pangilinan
normal voice, please.

He clears his throat
and tries again:

Today at lunch
In the courtyard
The Club Fair
Get involved!
Make a difference!
Make new friends!!!!!!!

He looks up from the sheet
and adds
(straight-faced)

Like Farters Anonymous!

Everyone chuckles, even me,
even our teacher
a little.

LUNCHTIME

The jasmine can wait
because I head
straight to the fair,
tables spread out
in a big U
and I go
to
every
single
one.

JUST DO

Club Fair has tables of
seventh and eighth graders
shouting things like
Join Us, We're the Best
passing out flyers
and mini candy bars.
They seem so much
older, taller
like we shouldn't be sharing
the same courtyard.

I start at one end

Athletics Association

    No thanks

Dungeons & Dragons Club

    Nope, that's okay

Chess Club
Page Turners
The Walkie-Talkies.

    Maybe
    Maybe
    Huh?

The next table has a handmade sign

Make It Yummy
Culinary Club

As soon as I walk up
two kids say:

We bake!
We cook!
We put on fun events!
I'm Amy!!!
Amy's got red hair
and grins the way she talks
—with multiple exclamation points.

And I'm Bill
says the kid next to her.
Bill's got dark hair
a name tag that says
8th grade, Student Council
and he waves and talks
to people like
he knows everyone.

What's your name?

      Isabel.

Just do it, Isabel.

He hands me a clipboard, a pen,

so I do.

What's your favorite cuisine? Bill asks.

I haven't tried much
outside of Filipino dishes
but whenever I flip
through cookbooks
there's a lot I want to try.

Ummm . . . everything?

Nice.

*In Culinary Club no one cares
if your challenges
don't come out
the way you want
as long as you tried.*

*Come to our
first meeting
tomorrow
BYOL
(Bring your own lunch)*

*Or not! says Amy.
We eat lunch family style
our club advisor is Mrs. Kapoor
and she always brings extra.
Anyway
we cook
we share.
Life is a tasty ride!!!*

I can tell her smile is
real.

My mind goes straight to
what I'd cook or bake
bibingka cakes wrapped in banana leaves
syrupy taho thick with soft tofu
banana turon to crunch into
every sweet, sticky bite.

My mouth waters.

But
I don't know what kids here like?

Still
now my mouth says *Sure*
and theirs say
See ya soon.

TEN MORE MINUTES

The bell hasn't rung
so I end up in my
new garden spot.

I grab water
from my lunch
pour the jasmine
a sweet, slow drip.
That's when I see
even the haircut I gave
has it looking better now,
maybe feeling better now.

Maybe it needed
a new person
to talk to
a kind face
to help it see
it still has
time
to grow.

MAYBE

I stroll the city
back to Auntie's
where Mama's with a lady
at the kitchen table
chatting like old friends.

Isabel, meet Auntie Delia.
We went to high school together.

Oh, Isabel. She smiles.
You look like your mom.

We've been catching up
says Mama.

And talking travel
adds Delia. The corners
of her eyes crinkle
as she smiles at me.

Delia owns a travel agency
Mama says before
they're back to talking.

So, as I was saying, Cora,
now's a great time to purchase
plane tickets.
Give me the dates
I'll do the rest.

Thank you, my friend.
We'll talk more later.

*I need to figure
a few things out.*

Does this have to do with
New York?

After Delia leaves I ask:

> *What was she talking about?*

Mama is
a wall of smiles.

*Nothing
I had some questions
about taking a trip.*

> *Where are you going?*

*Nowhere yet.
Just gathering info.
If it ends up as anything
I'll share.
But first
I was thinking
we haven't had much time
together
so what if
after Back-to-School Night
we have our own date,
you and me
on a school night.*
She smiles.

Is that something she did
with her nanny family?

I want to push more about
this plane ticket stuff
and what I heard on the phone
but she pulls me into
a warm hug and
I forget I'm irked

because

Her arms make me feel that

even if she misses her old family

maybe

she also misses me.

MARKET MEMORIES

The tiendaan was
a playground of
food and goods
sounds and smells
meat skewers
grilling
vendors
shouting

Taho!

My friends and I
would race through
the bustle.
I'd take pesos
from Mama's envelope
and buy taho for me,
Rosamie, Cristina.
A thick sticky mix of
silken tofu
tapioca pearls
scooped warm and sweet
the best cup of comfort
swirling in a
sugary brown syrup.

We'd roam the market
eating
gabbing

even though Lola
needed my help
selling
yelling

Jasmine!
    Sampaguita!

But it was snack time
running around time
talk about boys time
hanging out with friends time
the perfect kind of me time.

AT LUNCH THE NEXT DAY

I'm in the garden.
Not for the jasmine but for
Culinary Club.

LIKE AN OLD FRIEND

So happy you joined, Isabel!
Mrs. Kapoor says
clapping her hands.
The group's over there.
We usually meet in the kitchen
but on nice days we'll meet here.

I've liked all my teachers
—but especially her.

Would you like to see something fun?
She beckons me
to a familiar tree
standing tall and proud.

> *Oh, wow. Calamansi.*
> *It's huge!*

Full leaves
Branches brimming
with fruit.

I know calamondin's
common in the Philippines.
Thought I'd show you
one of the first trees
the Garden Club planted
many years ago.
The club's first advisor
was a lovely teacher
from the Philippines, too.

What happened to the club?

Not any interest lately.

She shrugs, yanks a green fruit
the size of a Ping-Pong ball
and throws it to me
for a perfect catch.

*If you ever need one
feel free to pick one.
Or ten!*
She laughs.

I bring it to my nose
inhale
its light tart scent.

First, the jasmine.
Now this.
Two things
here
from
home.

Some gardens
gift surprises.

INAUGURAL MEETING

Members sit in a circle
on tree stumps
Amy and Bill
faces from classes
everyone eating, snacking.
I'd never have the courage
to say hello around school
but here they seem friendly.

Until I spot them.

Melissa and Brandi,
and a few others from their clump
—minus Ashley.
I haven't seen them
with her at lunch anymore.

Amy waves me over
to an empty stump and
the breath in my chest

r e l e a s e s.

She leans in.

What do you like to bake?

I try to think up a good answer.

My eyes meet Melissa's.
My head fills with fear.

This fun chance
for new friends
has turned into
a thing
I might want
to flee.

THIS MEETING IS OFFICIALLY IN SESSION!

shouts Amy
and there's no more time
for any more worries
because she says:

I hereby announce
the first meeting
of the tastiest club
in the history of the
Bayview Bolts!

Every member
old and new
applauds, applauds.

Old chefs meet new chefs.
We'll tell you all about us.

One girl says
Get ready for some
ultimate cooking challenges.

One boy says
Every week there's a
make-at-home challenge, too.

Mrs. Kapoor says
We hold one big event
before winter break
to invite your families.
So start thinking about
what we'll plan.

Last time we did
Muffins with Mom
says Amy.

A hand raises
—Melissa's.

That's not really fair
for kids who don't have
a mom to bring.

You're absolutely right
says Mrs. Kapoor.
That's why I'd like you all
to keep brainstorming.

Amy pats a drumroll onto her thighs
and announces the first club challenge.

CUPCAKES!!!!!

Woooo! shouts Bill.

Your first
take-home challenge
is
to get your

CAKE

in a

CUP

ON.

Amy points to a table lined with
brown paper bags.
Grab one.
There's a cookbook
some basic ingredients.
Bake yours at home
add anything
to make yours
stand out.
Bring them on Friday.
Our club will be in the kitchen
for a special surprise challenge!

Neurons fire
bounce

explode.
Ideas launch
in fevered frenzy.

WHAT I'D RATHER DO

The meeting adjourns.
We gather and leave.

Mrs. Kapoor says to Amy and Bill
I keep thinking meeting outside
might inspire some of you to start
Garden Club again.
We used to do programs with
different community groups
like the senior center.
It would be lovely to
bring the garden back
hint, hint.
She nudges Bill,
who says

If I wasn't doing Tae Kwon Do Honor Society Recycling Rascals
The Brainy Bunch Mathletes Volleyball Cool Nerds and Soccer
and Basketball . . . then maybe.

I think you'll be fine
with your college applications,
Mr. Do-It-All
Amy says with a laugh.

Anyway
Seems like it would take
a ton of work
to bring this garden back
says Bill.

You're right.
Gardens take
time
soil
seeds
water
patience.
Definitely
a ton of work
I say.

Seems like you know a lot about gardens?
says Bill.

I nod. I tell them briefly
about my family
about our market business.
I don't show them
how the jasmine in the corner
is starting to look
not-so-bad.

Amy shoots laser eyes with
multiple exclamation points at me.

Isabel, you want to start it up?!!
You lead . . . I'll join.
We need more sixth-grade leaders,
you know, for when
this guy's off to high school next year.
She points to Bill with her thumb.

Do it! Awesome! We'll totally help!

says Bill and now
they're both beaming at me.

But I shake my head
a little shy and
tell them the truth:

*Baking cupcakes
sounds yummier than
growing vegetables.*

Amy shrugs.
Can't argue with that!

MAYBE YOU COULD HELP THEM

After school Mama meets me, curbside
—even though I've already
memorized the way home.
Seeing her
makes me excited
for our date tonight.

She's chitchatting with
a man.
I get closer and see
it's Melissa's dad, Eric.

Ah, Isabel,
I'm so happy to
finally meet your mom.

Melissa walks up.
Let's go, Dad.

But he says

Isabel, would you like
to hang out with Missy
after school sometime
—if you're okay with that?
he says to Mama.

Of course. I'd love for Isabel
to meet a new friend.

Why are they talking about me
like I'm not here?

You know, girls,
Lola Yoling and her friends
at the center keep asking
about you two.
They started their flowerpots.
Maybe you could help them.

For a second
my eyes meet Melissa's.
But . . . I have dance after school
she says to her dad.

Not every day, Missy.
I'll call you, Cora.

Mama nods and we leave
me wondering
what Melissa and I
would ever have
in common.

GOOD NEWS AND BAD

Mama says *I have*
good news and bad news
as we start our walk home.

> *Good news first.*

I've got a follow-up interview
at the hospital.
She looks at her watch.
In about forty-five minutes.

> *You do? That's great!*
> *But . . . the bad?*

Not bad-bad. Just that
I can't make the start of
Back to School Night.
Thankfully I found
Very Qualified Replacements.

We enter the house
and see Auntie and Joss,
Joss watching TV
all smiles when our eyes meet.

Back to School and *Date Night*
with my favorite tita and
new favorite cousin!
Hope it's okay I tag along?
Thought I'd say hi to
my old teachers.

I smile. *Mrs. Kapoor will love that.*

Mama says
I'll meet you all at school.
And Isa, we'll do
Our own little date
this weekend.

This isn't bad news,
just more times the fun.

MEET THE TEACHERS

At school we visit
every class, meet
every teacher
but by the end
Mama hasn't come.

Date Night starts
with disappointment
in a cute bakery
without her.

DATE NIGHT FOR THREE

If there's anything that
cheers me up
it's a scrumptious baked good.

We look through the
window displays
with hungry smiles.

Those cupcakes and cookies
look amazing
says Auntie.
What'll it be, gals?

Auntie gets a croissant
so flaky and buttery.
I get a cinnamon roll
gooey and yummy.

Joss points to
puff pastry circles
with whipped cream.
I share what I learned
from a cookbook
—that cream puffs
were once called
nun farts.

They laugh and
I brighten as
we eat.

I know
the imagination
the concentration
these sweets took to make.
Like little acts
of love.

I WANT TO SHOW YOU SOMETHING

Auntie and I drop off Joss
and get back just before Mama,
who bursts through the door.

Oh my goodness,
I'm so sorry,
I ran so late!

Does that mean the interview went well?
smiles Auntie.

Really, really well,
And I wrapped up
the other thing, too
she says, looking to my aunt
with a secret smile
before looking to me.

Isabel, let's take a walk.
I have something to show you.
The reason I'm late.

She extends her palm.
I go along
but don't accept
her hand.

THIS IS NOW

As evening settles
we stroll
stopping before
a five-story building.

Where are we?

Our new place!
Not the fanciest
but it's
cozy, clean
safe, ours.

Home.

HOME?

Isn't it exciting?
I don't have the keys yet
but had to show you.

I look up
at another new place
and wonder what's inside.

She said when
we came to California
she wanted our move
to be permanent
to start our new life, but
a small piece of me
hoped by
coming together
she would
take me back home and
stay.

Now I know.
This isn't temporary.

I sigh.

She doesn't see my sadness.
Her smile has stretched wider.

I can't believe we did it.
Hey, how about we tour
our new neighborhood?

REAL TALK

Down streets
past buildings, shops
until we reach school.

I can see the school's
tall calamansi tree
behind the gate.

School, the garden
it's so close
to the new apartment.

Let's sit a moment
Mama says and
we rest on a ledge.
What's wrong?

She can tell now
but doesn't know me
well enough to guess.

> I point to school.
> *I wanted you to at least*
> *meet Mrs. Kapoor tonight.*
> *She's my favorite teacher.*

I'm sorry, anak.
Tonight was the only time
to secure the apartment.
It had a long waitlist.

She sighs, too.

Mama looks toward the garden.

You know, Isa,
I miss home too.
When I was away
all those years
your lolo kept saying
to seek things
that felt familiar.
New York has gardens
like this, fenced in a city.
I gardened with the family's kids
every time I missed you
thinking of how you
were doing the same
with your grandfather.
It's why the family and I
gardened so much.

More words
more talk.

I'm trying to understand
but
it's hard.

Her face perks up.
Let's try to be excited.
Please.

New roots. Fresh start.

SUDDENLY, AN IDEA

Past her shoulder
I scan the garden
and spot my
lunchtime jasmine project.

I used to think
Mama didn't miss home
—all those pictures she sent
of gardens and snow.

I can see
even far away
the jasmine
looks a bit more green
stands a bit more proud.

The trimming I did
the water I gave
helped? I think?

It wasn't gone.
It only needed

new roots, a fresh start.

QUESTION FOR MAMA

I ask

     Does the apartment have a garden?
     You said we could grow
          Jasmine
               Sampaguita
     once we have our own place.

She shakes her head. *Sorry, Isa.*

     A balcony?

She smiles, but shakes her head again.

That doesn't mean
we can't grow plants
indoors. The apartment
has so much good light.

Up close
Mama looks older
than I remember.
Wrinkles cupping her eyes
gray hairs blending
into her black ones.

Whenever she sent pictures
I only saw
the fun
those kids
the new places

but never
the work
that sent me shoes
that bought me things
that brought me here.

My mom
she's trying hard.

Suddenly I get
an idea
for me
to try hard
for her.

HERE'S WHAT I'LL DO

I can do more than
bring the jasmine to life.
I can grow this whole garden
to remind us
both
of
home.
Especially if
here
is where we'll

stay.

GROW

GRANDMOTHERS KNOW

I'm up
it's early
I want to get to school
before the first bell rings.

First I grab the
gardening gloves
that Lola packed.

How'd she know
I'd need them?

EXECUTING THE PLAN

I let myself in through the
broken gate.

Yep. This place needs
a looooot of work.

That's when I spot
beyond the fence
two good faces.

> *Bill! Amy! Over here!*

They join me.

*Hey, Isabel,
what's up?*

> *Did you mean it when you said
> if I started a Garden Club
> you'd help?*

I show them
the bin
the tools.
I explain my idea to
bring this space
back to life.

> *We can garden
> as a club
> then eventually
> with the seniors.*

Bill rubs his hands
like he's kindling a fire.
You know what this means, Isabel?
Welcome to Presidents' Club!
A club for all the presidents of all the clubs!

Amy rolls her eyes.
He started that club last year.
Of course we'll help!
Exciting!

I'm in, says Bill, steely-eyed.

Grins.
High fives.
A plan:

   Meet back at lunch.

HARDER THAN I THOUGHT

Our first Garden Club meeting
has only three members
a few large planters
mostly empty.
There's old dirt
cracked earth
and when I try to
dig in a shovel it's
hard as rocks.

Put some muscle into it!
says Amy
but when she tries
nearly hurts herself.

Bill laughs
flexes his fake biceps
whomps in the spade
and same thing.
He winces.

> *Look, there's a hose*
> I say, trying it,
> water gushing out fine.

The whole lunch
we figure it out
tilling soil
spraying water.

People pass, peer in.
People point, poke fun.
Marcus Pangilinan walks by
cups his hands and shouts:

Nerds!

I wave back.

This dried-up plot
needs more arm strength
than three people.

We pause for a moment

> *What if we recruited help*
> *from all the good cooks?*
> I say.

Amy wiggles her fingers
a magical spell.
We could hold our
Culinary Club event
in our future garden!

And that's why you're
vice-prez of
Presidents' Club
says Bill to her.

Brilliant, I say.
Let's announce it
tomorrow at Club
after the Bake-at-Home Challenge.

TIME TO GO

When the last bell rings
I grab
my books
my backpack

   like everyone else.

No more
short-term intruder
here
as I fly
into the swarm

   like my new normal.

NEW THINGS

In a couple weeks
Mama and I will move
into our own place.

I'm beginning to know
my way around.
It's not hard
it's easy, a grid
I never wander far
just far enough
trying to spot the familiar
but mainly I see
new things
each time
like now
a plant store.

Through the windows
baskets cradling leafy waterfalls
flowers in a kaleidoscope of colors
covering tables, filling nooks.

The window has a painted sign:

California Dreaming

a border of orange flowers
like little cups of gold.
California poppies.

Lolo showed me their picture.
After the seeds ripen
the pod pops
sending seeds flying.
Each year they grow back.

A woman behind the window
gives a friendly wave.

One day I'll go in
but for now
time to get back
and get baking.

THE CULINARY CAPERS

In Auntie and Uncle's kitchen
in the brown bag
a copy of
The Culinary Capers: A Culinary Club Cookbook
recipes poems stories
stapled together
made by last year's members.

Table of Contents include:

    Bacon Me So Happy
    Chip Chip Hooray!

and one bonus comic strip

    Vegetrails: When Culinary Club Meets.

A page drawn with
silly-looking vegetables
pointing to Bayview Middle School.

The turnip says
Is there a turnip ahead?

The bean says
I dunno, I've never bean this way.

And the snap pea says
*Come on, we're late for the meeting and
I gotta pea!*

WHAT KIND OF CUPCAKES SHOULD I MAKE?

It's time to bake some good sweets
but put my spin on these treats.
I'm thinking calamansi
—a flavor that's more like me.

SIGNS

No calamansi
anywhere in the fruit bowl or fridge
so I set off with
an envelope in my pocket
a map in my head
a corner market
a few blocks down.

The produce section has
lemons and limes
oranges and grapefruit
but not what I need.

Across the way, another store
but still no calamansi,
only a curmudgeonly lady
who, after I ask,
says: *Cala-what?*
English only here!

I scurry out
relieved to escape
her grimace.

I can go for chocolate
or vanilla bean
but
that's when I remember!

My feet forge
back to school
to the garden
to the tree.

Found some.

THE FINAL BAKED RESULT

One tray for school
tomorrow
another tray for
now
for my host family
who after dinner
tastes the little cakes
(chocolate calamansi!),
Uncle saying with a happy smile
Isabel, anak
I knew you could bake
but I didn't know you could bake!

I've seen how
sweet treats bring out our best
because who can resist
something delicious
made with skill and
layered with love?

> I tell my aunt and uncle
> *These cupcakes are*
> *to thank you for*
> *helping us and*
> *housing us.*

We'll miss you when
you move
says Auntie.

We do a cupcake toast
and Mama says
this is a thankful celebration
of all good things to come.

TOMORROW

Before bed, Mama says
I talked to Melissa's dad,
and they'd love
to have you over tomorrow.

Melissa's not mean
like Ashley
but it's her dad
who invited me
—not her.
It doesn't seem
like she wants to be
friends.

I'd like to say
Can I think about it?
but Mama interrupts with *I told him*

yes.

It's okay.
This whole day
the garden
the baking
everything's feeling good.
Nothing's changing my mood.

HOW IT STARTS

Culinary Club
in a kitchen of
long silver tables
bowls and tools
ingredients galore.

So. Cool.

Each member's brought in
their cupcakes and we
discuss our bakes
dissect our process
like serious cupcakers.

One person filled her paper cups too high
and they turned out crispy,
still tasty (just not pretty).

Another added
salt not sugar (on accident).
The ultimate caketastrophe!

There's Rodrigo
who didn't start from scratch
he used a box mix (all he had)
but everyone shrugs
who cares.

Mrs. Kapoor's
walking around

checking our skills
saying
I hope you're all thinking
about what our
event this year
can be?

She looks at my work and says
Deliciously beautiful, Isabel!

Amy announces
Our Super-Secret Special Surprise . . .

...ICING CHALLENGE!!!!!

The old members bring out
Piping bags
Silver tips
Super professional and
So. Cool.

For health codes
we put on hairnets.

We all crack up.

HOW IT ENDS

Mrs. Kapoor demonstrates
on some red velvet (yum)
precise and focused
a perfect swirl
Voilà!

She waves her hands around.
*Everyone find a station
and get icing.*

Melissa, Brandi, and their pals
spread out at a table and
so does their laughter
but I don't feel left out.

I start with a star tip
and chocolate frosting.
My first one's lopsided.
Second one's neater.
Third one is

Oh My Yum!

Like a cupcake in a fancy bakery window!

I want to show Amy
so I pick it up
delicately,
but when I turn around
quickly

I smack into Melissa
(on accident).

The brown icing clumps onto
her bright white shirt.

My new shirt!

Oh no.

Heads whip our way.
Brandi runs up with napkins
but instead of helping
it smears around.

Please, stop
Melissa says.
You're making it worse.

She runs off.

Everyone's back to piping.
Because who can resist
a good icing challenge!

Almost like it didn't happen

except I know it did.

ONLY THEIR FEET

Midway through last class
I ask for the bathroom pass.

My footsteps tap
down an empty corridor
lined with blue lockers
echoing in the quiet.
For a moment
with no one around
I can breathe.

In the bathroom there's one person
in a closed stall next to mine
I see only their feet
—black Converse.

When Lola used to cut the tips of my shoes
long before Mama's checks
I wanted sneakers
but sandals looked better cut off
like it was an actual style.

I wash up
stare at myself in the mirror
seeing the mom I don't know yet
with her shallow-set eyes
and the dad I've never met yet
though people who knew him said
I have his dimpled chin.

I wonder if that's true
and I wonder
when I see myself
like this
who I'm really looking at.

MIRROR MIRROR

There I am
there and here
curiously looking
always wondering
cautiously questioning
boldly daydreaming
reflecting
daydreaming boldly
questioning cautiously
wondering always
looking curiously
here and there
Am I there?

HELPING A STRANGER

From the stall with the Converse
crying
breaks my daydream.

I dry up
pause and
listen.

> *Are you okay?*

Not sure who's crying
but someone answers
sniffly, so softly
that even if I *did* know
those shoes
I don't recognize the voice.

Are there . . .
. . . any pads in the machine?

I check the silver box.

> *It's out.*
> *But hold on.*
> *Just wait.*
> *I'll be right back.*

I run out
slip back to class
where they're
busy sticking

toothpicks into marshmallows
building sound structures.

Lola told me to
always keep a
pad in my pack.

I grab it
run out
jut my hand
under the stall.

THIS IS ACTUALLY HAPPENING

Final bell rings
I make my way
through the crush of people
until I'm stopped by
Melissa
Brandi at her side
blocking me
shielding the sun.

They're the only ones
in their little clique
who haven't said anything
or done anything
directly mean to me
but I guess there's
a first time for everything
—especially after
Today's Shirt Incident.

I brace myself.

But Melissa says:

Isabel,
you're coming over, right?

YES OR NO?

No death stare
but her face is
unreadable.

Melissa looks to her real friend.

Can you come, too, Brandi?

*I have Korean school
but I'll walk home with you*
Brandi says.

        What's that? I ask.

*I'm part Korean so
my parents make me
go learn about
my culture.*

Not sure if I'd ever need
a special school
to learn about Filipino Me.

Melissa's glancing around.

So you want to come over?

A dare, maybe?
But the truth comes out:

My dads said to invite you.

In my head
Lolo and Lola's voices
saying how a new friend
is like a new gift.
It's why at the market
everyone knew them.
They treated all customers
kindly, fairly
so they always had
repeat customers.

I surprise myself:

      Sure.

I can tell by their expressions
they didn't think I'd say that.

THE INTRUDER

After school
We walk with
Brandi in the middle.

They pause
in front of a building
for a secret friendship handshake
of fist bumps and palm slaps
the way Cristina and I used to,
laughing so hard by the end
I have to turn my head
because I feel like I
don't belong in their song.

See ya! Brandi yells out.

Melissa's face says she's
still not sure about this.

Well, I've got some news:

    Same here.

SOME HAVE MORE THAN ONE

It doesn't take long
to reach her house.
She leads me to
a brightly painted
purple-ish one
white trim like cake icing
blooms in pots that line the walk.

Very San Francisco.

We tromp in.
Stairs swoop up
into the house
where sunlight hits the floors
and a curved window overlooks
people playing tennis at a park.
Blue skies
bright clouds
—like a view from
one of Mama's pictures.

She slings down her bag and
I'm not sure
what to do
what to say
where to sit
how to move
so I do what she does
—put my bag on the floor

shove my hands in my pockets
and stare everywhere
except at her.

Be right back, she says

leaving me.

Why did I agree to come over again?

Someone bounds down,
a friendly-faced guy.

You must be Isabel! Hi, Isabel!

A grin like he just enjoyed
ice cream,
light hair and skin
definitely not Filipino.

I'm Melissa's dad John.

I've got two
she explains, rejoining us,
her whole outfit changed
a new shirt and shorts
—neither with icing.

She gives her second dad
a big bear hug like the one
she gave her first dad.

I used to wonder
about my father

who he was
why I didn't have one.
But I had what I needed.
Grandparents like parents
their big bear hugs
that squish out
my worries
my wonders.

I don't wonder anymore.
Only in times like this
when I see that
some kids have two dads
while others have none.

UNEXPECTED TASTE OF HOME

Hey, girls, how about an after-school snack?

My dad's a chef.
Come on.

The kitchen's so big
my old house would fit inside.
It's so bright and light.
I can almost hear Lola's
wide-eyed appreciation
her high-pitched
Ay nako!
—if she even saw just a picture
of this spacious place.

Sadness pings.
I wish my grandparents
could see all the new things
I've been seeing.
But that's gone
when I notice on the counter
a single savory dish
smelling of
home,
activating every taste bud.

Melissa pulls out
three plates, three forks
and we sit around

their massive counter
scooping rice
ladling chicken afritada,
afritadang manok,
tucking in.

Not as good as Lolo's
(which is not as good as mine),
but I'm licking my lips
at the garlicky comfort of
tomatoes and potatoes
in a thick, rich stew.

I've been trying to cook more
Filipino food
says her non-Filipino dad.

It's my favorite
says Melissa.

    Mine, too.

I always want to
lick the plate clean
but my parents say it's rude
she whispers to me
and I know what she means.
I used to try but
Auntie Flor would shake her head
and say that's not what a
Little Miss Ilocos Sur
would do.

We devour our snack
then Melissa licks her plate
and laughs.

He can't get mad
if we both do it!
So I do.
John joins, too.
Kind of weird
kind of fun
we're all busting up.

Okay, girls, go play!

We're hanging out, Dad,
not playing.
She rolls her eyes.

Okay, girls, go hang!
says John, shooing us out,
and here I am again
with this girl again
who said she didn't like me
not to my face
but *on* her face
only now she's inviting me
upstairs to see her room.

QUIZ TIME

This room is not Friendly Fun
more like Perfectly Perfect.
A pink-and-gray bed
two pink-and-purple beanbags.

My eyes try to take it all in
without seeming too obvious.

I've wondered about
rooms like this
girls like her
kids in big houses.

Melissa sits on her bed.
Maybe Mama's life
felt like this.

I sink myself into
a designer beanbag.

What now?
She grabs a magazine
from her nightstand.
I know, let's take a quiz!

WHICH GIRL ARE YOU?

If you don't really know,
take this quiz to find out.

When you're with your friends how do you act?

> Her: We mess around and act awesome
> Me: Have fun and act silly

During lunch, would you rather

> Her: Hang out with friends
> Me: Volunteer to pick up litter around school

What's your favorite movie genre?

> Her: Drama
> Me: Comedy

How would your friends describe you?

> Her: Amazing
> Me: Ambitious

If you could travel anywhere in the world, where would you want to go?

> Her: Paris
> Me: New York

What's your dream job?

> Her/Me: Chef/Baker

I'll tally.
She marks it up.
You got: Forever Friend
I got: Teen Drama!
What?!?!

We crack up.

> *Let me see.*

She hands me the magazine
I scan our results.

> *Actually . . .*
> *I think we're both . . .*
> *. . . Youniquely You.*

We eye each other.

I like it.

> *Same here.*

QUIZ MACHINES

These quizzes
don't always get stuff right.
She flings the magazine.

For some reason
this gets us asking
more questions:

Favorite pizza?
Celebrity crush?
Favorite song?
Do aliens exist?
Things our parents do that we hate?

I can't complain
my dads are pretty great
she says, a small smile.
What's your dad like?

                    Never met mine.

I never met my mom.
My dads took me home
from the Philippines
when I was a baby.

                    Have you ever gone back?

No, but they're taking me
after eighth-grade graduation.

Whenever Auntie Flor would gossip
about people from our town
like the mothers
who left their daughters
Lolo would scold her
saying
everyone has a story
you just don't know
what it is.

I guess we all
have our own
stories.

JUST LIKE THAT

It's quiet now.

> *Gonna go now*
> I say and start to get up.
> *And . . . I'm sorry.*
> *About your shirt. Earlier.*

It's okay.
It was an accident.
And I'm sorry too
about that bottle
Ashley spilled.
She looks at me.
What was in it?

I think about sharing
but don't want to get laughed at.
Sure we hung out but
that doesn't mean
we're friends.

> *It was . . . something . . . from home.*

Oh.

You know, I'm not
friends with Ashley anymore.

> *You're not?*

She thinks she's better
than everyone.
Brandi and I got tired of it.

Oh.

I thought I wanted
to be popular but
not like that.
Anyway, thanks for
helping me earlier.

      What are you talking about?

In the bathroom
with the pad.

That was her?

I'd just gotten it
I wasn't sure what to do
I was too embarrassed
to go back to class.

      The same thing
      kind of happened to me
      my first period.

I share
at school
too embarrassed to tell anyone
so I wrapped my jacket
around my waist
until Lola saw my stained pants
and showed me what to do.
I never even told Mama
I'd finally gotten it
—although Mama never asked.

And just like that
we talk
about friends
about school
about my old friends at my old school.

My first hangout
without my friends from home
us sipping calamansi lemonade
in Lolo's garden
a bit sweet
a bit sour.

After a bit
I get up for real.

> *See you at school.*

Yeah. See ya.

A PLACE TO BELONG

I'd known Rosamie
my whole life but
met Cristina in
the garden at school
when we were little.

I'd walked by
saw her crying
I stopped and asked

    What's wrong?

She was new
had no friends
so I sat
ate my lunch
let her cry.

She stayed quiet
wouldn't talk
I grabbed a watering can
and did my thing.

She watched me
I showed her what to do
until finally
she helped.

That night
I'd told my lola

what happened
and she
looked at me
so proud
and said
green spaces
are where
anyone can
connect

are where
anyone can
belong.

PHASE I

The next morning
at school
Bill's taping up a sign
in the courtyard
the school's heart
for everyone to see:

Thyme to Turnip the Beet
Garden Club
Meet Tomorrow at Lunch
Come Grow with Us
Let's Bring Our Garden Back to Life!

PHASE II

Culinary Club
converges in the kitchen.
Even though it's lunchtime
it's Breakfast Week.

Half the kitchen is
Team Omelet
the other half
Team Fluffy Scrambled Eggs.
I look down at my runny attempt.
Team Try Again.

Amy leans into me
while sprinkling chives.
I'll make the announcement
that you're
going to make an announcement.

> *But they'll listen to you more.*

But you're Madam Garden Club Prez!

She rolls her eyes and says
Fine but you'll need to
work on it.
It's what leaders do.
And you're a good leader, Isabel.

She beams the same smile
that made us friends.

ATTENTION, MEMBERS!!!

Are you interested in the perfect pairing of
food and gardening?
If so, join
the Gardening Club!
Our Culinary Club is
every other day
so you can alternate.
We want to
bring back the garden
and hold our
Culinary Club events there.

Mrs. Kapoor smiles at me.

I work up the nerve and yell

      Who's in?

A couple hands raise
but everyone's back to
going gourmet with goat cheese.
At least we're trying,
waiting and seeing.

      A twelve-hour plane ride.

      Mama.

      Seeds to sprout.

I know how to wait by now.

ROLL WITH IT

Walking home
After school
I hear wheels
getting louder
scratching pavement.
A blur streaks by
topped by a pink helmet
a poof of curls
peeking out.

Brandi.

She jumps it
sticks it
lands.
She zooms right up.

How'd you learn that?

A lot of falling on my butt.
Ever ridden one?

Gosh. No.

Wanna try?

Is it hard?

She grins like she's in
a toothpaste commercial.

Only at first.

A SMALL PUSH

Next to us, a park.
Shady trees
winding paths.

We enter.

I slip on her helmet
stand on the board
all wobbly and
jump off
immediately.

       Can't
Can.

She gives a small push and I
roll
slowly
shakily
until I let go.

INVITATION

I hop off
and we walk
and we talk
about how she wanted to join
Tarot Card Club with Ashley
but it's the same day as
Culinary Club with Melissa
so she had to choose.

We reach her building.

I walk off.
She calls out:

Hey, Isabel,
I'm having a sleepover
next weekend.
Can you come?

I look to my
left and right
no one
no joke
just us.

Me, a nod, a

> *maybe.*
> *I'll ask.*

Her, a thumbs-up.

WHAT I'M WONDERING

When I get to the house
that travel agent lady, Auntie Delia,
is at the front door.

Hello, sweetie!
Is your mom home? I've been knocking.
She was supposed to meet me
at my office a little while ago.
Thought I'd stop by. Maybe she forgot.

> I shake my head.
> *She's at work, Auntie.*

Shoot. I have something for her travels.
She taps an envelope.

Her travels?

Know when she'll be back?

> *Want me to . . . give it to her?*

Say yes, say yes
so I can look.
Are they tickets for New York?
That girl Nicolette keeps calling, calling.

It's all right. I'll reach her later
and she's off with a shrug.

I need to find out
what was in that

envelope.

MOVING DAY

A new place looks like
movers carrying a couch,
a table, two beds.

A new kitchen tastes like
Mama and me eating Chinese takeout
with some aunties and Joss.

A new bedroom looks like
me gazing out a window
no gardens, only buildings.

A new apartment doesn't feel like
a home yet.
Still just a place to live.

OVER BEEF WITH BROCCOLI

I whisper to my cousin
What's a slumber party like?
I never did that at home
—not sure if I want to go.

WHAT HAPPENS AT SLEEPOVERS
(ACCORDING TO COUSIN JOSS)

Talking about
boys
kisses
crushes

Playing the game
light as a feather stiff as a board
where you'll lie down
your friends will say a chant
and you! Will! Actually! Levitate!
That or Ouija board.

Eating
all the snacks

Staying
up all night

Making
friends for life.

Just don't
say the wrong things
bring stuffed animals like a baby
be the first girl to fall asleep
let them know you've never been to a sleepover before
because they'll think you're not cool!

Hello, butterflies.
Giant mutated ones.

HOUSEWARMING GIFTS

Auntie Grace hands me two things: *For you, Isabel.*
First the twins' hamburger phone to call home and tell
your grandparents, who miss you, that you are quite well.
Plus a box from your lola, I love the sweet smell.

ALL THIS WAY

I thank Auntie
for the phone
and the box.

Of course, anak.
And here, for you, too.

She hands me a calling card.

I know sometimes
it's just nice to call home
whenever you want.

I give back
a huge smile
a huge hug.

I can smell Lola's
jasmine perfume
on the small box
like a small hug
all this way
from home.

Mama and I say our
thanks and goodbyes.
I take the box
into my new room
to find out
what it holds.

WHAT'S INSIDE

My grandmother
reaches me through
her sweet scent
her sweet letter
her sweet candies.

There's also
a photo of Lolo
a message scrawled on the back

Look closely, my Isa.
Do you spot it?

I study it and see
his smile, but also
a planter
with buds
—no blooms.
Is that . . . Jazzy?
My little plant
that wasn't
surviving, thriving?
It must be!

This whole box.
The sign
I needed.

BACK BY BOX

Now it's my turn.
From my new room
a different box
an empty one
for people I miss.

I'm filling it with
love and longing
a way to connect from afar.

For Cristina and Rosamie
strawberry Airheads
Sassy and *Seventeen*
shimmery lip gloss.
A lip gloss for Lola
A book for Lolo
and seed packets, too,
of California poppies.
I don't know if
they'll grow there
but I do know
he'll love them.

I see why Mama would do this.
It's not so easy to fly home.
I don't know
when I'll see them again
if I'll see them again
so for now this is a bridge

helping me say hello
connecting me
from home to home.

Pasalubong means gift
a tradition
Filipinos homesick and heartsick
sending themselves
back by balikbayan box
so when their loved ones
open it they'll touch the things they've touched
all those miles away.

My loved ones will see
a postcard
a Golden Gate Bridge
some words
neatly printed

    I miss you.

NO GOING BACK

Late-night knocking
Mama at my door.
Late-night talking
Mama on my bed.

I put Lola's box aside.
She glances around at
basic furniture
barren walls.

If this room was a quiz it would be
Blank Slate.

Needs a little color, huh?

She's smiling but does
that sighing thing
her exhale
heavy and deep
the kind she'd give Lola
sharing her problems late at night
when they thought I couldn't hear.

I'm sorry we don't have
our own garden yet.
But we'll bring in plants
we'll decorate the walls
we'll make this place
our own.
Right?

I try to smile.

I'm sorry you hate it here.
This may not feel like
home
but it does to me.
Because we're together.

Her warm hand on my cheek.

I smile. A real one.

I see how that settles her.
Shoulders relaxing.
Face untensing.

I know
what Mama's done,
how she's saved
how we have more
because of how she sacrificed.

I'll keep trying for her.
For us.

     Right.

Maybe
I don't need to bring
home
near.

Maybe
I should
make my home
wherever I am.

BEFORE SCHOOL

I pull open
a drawer
I pull out
a box
the one Lola
slipped into my suitcase
with the seeds
Mama had sent
long ago
that I'd never
wanted
or needed
until
now.

GARDEN TIME

At school the day drags
but finally it's lunchtime.
I hope people come.

READY FOR PLANTING

I enter the dried-up old space
ready to lead.
Madam Garden Club Prez
has a nice ring
but there's no one here
only three novice gardeners
(including me).
Maybe people are still eating?

Amy, Bill, and I
scarf down our lunches
then get
moving
      moving
            moving.

      Let the weeding begin! says Bill.

Still, no one.

Doesn't matter.
We yank on gloves
and turn into
weeding machines.

That's when I see
a few Culinary Club kids.

Can we help? asks one of the girls.

Awesome, I say.

More gloves for
more hands for
weeding
        sweeping
                pruning.

That's when I see
Melissa and Brandi
ready to literally
dig right in.
We keep going
all lunch long.
Bill even finds
packets of seeds
in the bin.
Should we plant them?

        Let's get the soil ready first.

By the time
we're done
we have
a fresh plate
a clean slate.

LAST STEP

I bring out
the seed packets
the ones from Lola
plus the ones Bill found.

Everyone puts up their palms
I shake a few out
we each find a pot.

Some water
Some sun
Some love.

We'll see how they do.

APPROVAL

Right before
lunch finishes
Mrs. Kapoor pops in
looks around
wide-eyed
bright-eyed
all smiles.

Congratulations.
You have yourself
a new club.

So much for
no one has to know.

NEIGHBORHOOD SURPRISES

Isabel! Wait up!

Melissa's walking home.
She gives me a grin.
That was fun today.

I grin back.

We near that plant store
across from the senior center
and put our noses
to the glass.

Let's go in
she says,
swinging open the door
so we can't change our minds.

A NICE PLANT OR SOMETHING

Why, hello! croons a lady
and I can tell she's the owner
—with dirt under her nails and
tanned arms like she's been out
in a garden all day.
Definitely a Plant Lady.
The same woman who
smiled at me the first time
I saw this store
from the outside.

What can I do you kids for?

> *Just looking.*

Everywhere we turn
is every emerald hue.

I have one of Mama's envelopes
with a little money left over.
I tell Melissa:

> *Let's buy something for*
> *Lola Yoling and the others*
> *for their patio.*
> *Then we can tell them*
> *how we're restarting the garden!*

Perfect.

See anything you like?
asks the Plant Lady.

I'm looking for a nice plant
for our friends across the street.

Oh, the seniors?
A lot of them
come in to browse.

She walks to a table and
reaches for a container
full of pointy leaves
pinks, greens,
maroons, yellows.

A Coleus Rainbow,
or Painted Leaves.
Good indoors, outdoors.

She hands it to me.

How much?

For those kind people?
Not a thing.

WE HEAD OVER

Out we go
plant in hand
enjoying the day
thinking about
how friendships
are weird.
You don't know someone
across the world
then suddenly
you do.

We look both ways
to cross the busy street.
That's when we hear

      a scream

That's when we hear

      Help!

That's when we see outside the center

      A crowd
      A commotion

Once the traffic clears
we sprint across.

WHAT HAPPENED?

Lola Yoling's crying
Lolo Frank's lying down
staff's hovering
everyone's concerned.

He was robbed
I hear someone say.

My hands around
the potted plant
shake.

     Is he okay?

Girls, stand back, please
says someone who works there
as an ambulance siren nears.

WILL HE BE OKAY?

Melissa and I
try to look
but
chaos.

What just happened?

Auntie spots us.
Girls? What are you doing here?

Will Lolo be okay?
asks Melissa.
Her eyes are watering.

Her dad comes over.
Come on, girls,
let's get you both home.
We follow him
to the car,
me still holding
the leafy rainbow mix.

WHAT AND WHY

The next morning
Mama and I stop by
Auntie and Uncle's
to grab the rest of our things.

Uncle's at the table
with a paper,
searching for information
about Lolo Frank.

I don't see anything
he says
until finally
a short article
a teeny square
buried in back
not front-page news.

73-year-old man
robbed at the
Asian American Senior Center
he reads
snaps the paper
shakes his head.

Money stolen
elderly man assaulted
shaken and confused
but okay. Released
from the hospital.

So scary, says Mama.

I know. I was told
he's fine now
says Auntie.
Mainly bruises.
And scars from
this memory,
probably.
A scare for everyone.

It's happened before
says Uncle,
still flipping through
again
as if he's not satisfied
with the little he found.

        It has? I say.

That lolo
he's someone's dad
somebody's son
just a kind, older man.

Why would anyone do that to him?

I wish I knew, Isabel
says Auntie.
It's a shame.
People see them
as easy targets? I guess?
For money, their age

the shape of their eyes.
They've never done
anything wrong.
I will never understand.

Uncle puts the paper down.
That building needs more security,
a guard, cameras.

The center's working on it.
Not so cheap and easy
says Auntie
her own sigh heavy.
We've voiced our concerns
with the city,
and taken action
but sometimes,
I don't know,
it's like

we're invisible.

NO ONE'S TALKING ABOUT IT

The morning bulletin
read by Marcus
with not one mention
of the robbery.

Science class with Melissa.
My dad says Lolo's better
she tells me but then
turns back to her friends.

Math class I ask our teacher
if she'd heard the news.
Oh goodness, how awful
but then back to algebraic equations.

I go through the day and
all I see are
smiling faces
no one pausing
everyone going about
like no one knows
or worse
like no one cares.

Like it never even happened.

WORDS FOR INVISIBLE

Imperceptible

Microscopic

Not in sight

Not the same

Unappreciated

Unrecognized

Unnoticed

Unobserved

Unseeable

Unseen.

SLEEPING OVER

My first American
slumber party.
My first slumber party
ever.

Mom drops me off
and meets Brandi's nice mom,
who tells me

Just up the stairs, honey

as Mama waves goodbye.

I look up
Voices travel down
The laughter gets louder.

I remember that first day
and all their laughing.
Maybe this is a mistake.
I think about turning around
but Mama's gone.

Too late to leave now.

LOUD DOOR

I knock.
No answer.
I push it open.

A pillow factory
exploded.

Everyone's
on cozy cushions
and fuzzy blankets.
Music blares from a
silver boom box.
The Spice Girls.
A memory.
Me and Rosamie and Cristina
lip-syncing
Tell me what you want
what you really really want
in between bursts of laughter.

I only know a few faces.
The chatter stops.
They all stare.

What if I say
all
the
wrong
things?

LOUD LUNGS

Hi

I manage

then someone squeals
someone else shouts
Isabel! Isabel's here!
It's Brandi
linking our arms
bringing me into
the frantic fold
until soon we're all
squealing and screaming
talking and sharing
snapping gummy worms
painting our nails
listening to songs.

Let's play Truth or Dare!
someone yells
and they all shriek
me included
as loud as our lungs will go.

CAUTION

My cousin warned me:
*Whatever you do make sure
that you don't get picked.*

DARE

My slumber party
so my choice
who goes first
says Brandi.

She closes her eyes
points
moves her arm back and forth
like a sprinkler.
Girls jump
like hot kernels.

Yoooooooooooooooooooooooou're . . .

IT!

The finger points
to Robin.

Robin
steely-eyed
makes her decision.

DARE.

OKAY, LET ME THINK

Brandi
taps
her
chin.

Go to my big sister Jada's room
steal her bra
and put it
in the freezer!

Hysterics.
Laughing hyenas.

My sister hates
her stuff being touched
so if she catches you
you're
dead.

DEAD.

THE MISSION

Stealthily,
Robin sneaks into
Jada's room
tears through drawers
flings out socks
us standing guard
until she finds
a pink cotton bra
a little flower in the center
the cups way bigger than mine
and we follow Robin

      padding
            down
                  the
                      stairs

where Jada's watching TV
with Brandi's little twin brothers
Mitch and Matt.
In one smooth move
we sneak as a clump
to the kitchen
Robin yanks the freezer open
throws the bra inside and
whomps the door closed.

WE DID IT

Quiet high fives

until

we

see

Jada

standing at the doorway

hands on her hips

mad and mean

and we scream

scream

scream.

WHO'S NEXT?

Back in Brandi's room
Robin does the pointing
and now
the
finger
lands
on
me.

ME.

Pick your poison.

Oh, wow.

I scan their faces
then spit it out.

TRUTH

Okay, let me think
says Robin
grinning, scanning,
more chin tapping.

She looks directly at me.

What was in that bottle
on the first day of school?
The one Ashley spilled.

The screaming's stopped
the sugar's dropped
now it's head resting
pillow sinking
deep thinking
—every eye on me.

WHAT I TELL THEM

I find my strength and say

> *It was my grandma's.*
> *It wasn't perfume.*
> *I mean, it could be.*
> *It's for me*
> *for whenever I . . .*
> *feel a little anxious.*
> *To smell.*

To smell what? someone asks.

> *Home.*

They look at me
puzzled faces
wide-eyed
so I tell them
how I lived in the Philippines
and had to move

> here.

They look at me
Wide-eyed
curious faces
so I tell them
how my mother left
but she's back now

> yet somehow not back.

They look at me
curious faces
wide-eyed
and more pours out
a rushing hose

How I miss my old friends

      How I've never been to a slumber party

How I feel so bad for what happened to Lolo Frank

      How different I feel than everyone at school but

How somehow, too, I'm getting used to things.

They watch me
intently
and I realize
my face
it's wet
I'm crying.

I've let everything flow
even though
they didn't ask to know
this much.

Oh no.

I'm so embarrassed.

Can't believe I just did that.

HOW IT SHOULD FEEL

The room's quiet,
girls hugging pillows.
If they're still watching me
I wouldn't know.
I'm staring at my lap.

Brandi says
I'm sorry about what Ashley did, Isabel.
It's why I didn't invite her.

Yeah, chime in the others.
We don't know why she's so popular.

I'm sorry, too
says Melissa
if I ever acted
weird.
Ashley's the one
who said I shouldn't
be friends with you.

We look at each other.

But . . .
I'm glad you moved.
And I'm glad you came to the party.

I look around now
some girls are watching me
some girls are not

and somehow
it all feels okay
not as embarrassing.
Maybe how
making friends
should feel.

THE WAY IT HITS

Robin says,

Can I tell you what the dare was?

Oh no, says Melissa,
anticipating
who knows what.

It was

to

French-

kiss

a

pillow

like it's

Marcus Pangilinan.

Every girl
bubbles up
light and laughter.

Melissa takes her pillow
and whacks Robin.
So does Brandi.

The door opens.
A shower of
spongey Ping-Pongs
pellet us from Mitch and Matt
bouncing off walls
unexpectedly
the way
friendship
sometimes
hits.

PAST MIDNIGHT

We stay up
ears dense with laughter
bellies full of snacks
until one by one
they drop
like flies.

Except for me.

I lie in the dark
feeling fine
for once
about leaving
there for here.

LATE-NIGHT IDEAS

Everyone's asleep
until I hear a sigh
one sleeping bag over.

Melissa.

She grabs the flashlight
shines a spotlight
on the ceiling.
We both look up.

I still feel bad, too,
you know, about
what happened to Lolo Frank.

She props up
on an elbow.
She shares
how she's gotten
to know the seniors
because of her dad,
and how she's heard
all their stories about
their families
their happiness
their hard moments, too.

They're like my
own grandparents.
That's what they
feel like to me.

Actually
that's what
all older Filipinos
feel like to me.
Like I know them
—even when I don't.
Is that weird?

    Not weird.

Two of us
sighing in the dark
now.

    I wonder
    if there's a way
    we can help them?

She shines the light on my face
an interrogation
or a spotlight.
She turns it off.

    Hold on. Do that again.

Do what?
Then once more
a bright circle
reaching my eyes
shining a light.

    I think I know a way.

HOW WE CAN HELP THEM

I whisper

> *What if we*
> *raised money*
> *for the center?*
> *Culinary Club*
> *+*
> *Garden Club*
> *combine them*
> *in the garden*
> *like we planned*
> *but make it a fundraiser.*
> *We'll garden.*
> *We'll sell*
> *delicious baked goods.*
> *Donations and proceeds*
> *all for the senior center.*
>
> *We'll shine a light on*
> *what happened to Lolo.*

Melissa sits up, shouts
I love it!

Be quiet!
whisper-hisses one of the girls
and Melissa plops down.

We plot in the dark
until my eyes grow heavy

and the next thing I know
I smell pancakes and
we're waking to morning.

THE ULTIMATE PLAN

A garden for my mom
A garden for the school
A garden for the seniors

A place where we all belong.

THE NEXT MORNING

Melissa and I
walk toward home.
First stop
the senior center.
First question
How's Lolo Frank?

The lolas crowd us with hellos
and Lola Yoling says
Ask him for yourself, girls
as she walks with Lolo
arm in arm.

I take Lolo's hand
raise it to my forehead in
a mano po
a sign of respect
for my elders.

We sit on the patio.
Lolo explains how
out of nowhere
someone demanded his wallet.

I was so scared.
I gave him my money
and he ran.

Your lolo would have
run after him

if he didn't have
such bad knees
says Lola Yoling.

Or . . . not
he says, chuckling
and this makes everyone laugh.

> *I'm glad you're okay, Lolo.*

So am I.
But you know, anaks,
I have been scared before.
So much more than this.
And though it's not easy
I've always gotten through it.

He shares his memories
as a soldier in World War II
marching in the Bataan Death March
only a boy, age
twenty-one
trudging
sixty-six
grueling miles with
no food and no water
only his family waiting
wondering, worried.

He shares his memories of
when he came here
leaving Lola

with their daughters
in their homeland,
not knowing if he'd bring them over
not knowing if he'd ever see them again.

I worked on a ship in Alaska.
I flew on a plane by myself
for the first time to get here.

> *So did I,* I say
> and he asks for my story.

The lolos and lolas
listen intently
as I speak
nod their head
like they know.

Lolo Frank pats my hand.
And now, like me, Isabel
you can get through
anything.

BEFORE WE GO

We wanted to tell you that
we're holding a fundraiser
for all of you here at the center
so that we can get
the senior/school garden program
going again.
A place where we
can all hang out
says Melissa.

We share the details
and invite them all.

> *You don't even have to garden.*
> *You can just come*
> *eat yummy stuff.*
> I smile.

Oh, girls!
Lola Yoling claps her hands.

Sounds perfect. Thank you
says Lolo Frank, who
pats my hand
then pats Melissa's.
His knuckles and wrinkles
like stories.
A bridge.

FEELING THANKFUL

Sometimes, when Lolo
would walk me through
his garden
we'd pause at trees
to look for buds,
the ones that waited
dormant all winter.
They always seemed
a surprise,
but he'd say

No, look closely
the buds are already there
getting ready to
open.
You just didn't
notice until
now.

TREES CAN TALK

When they're distressed
by disease or drought

they release chemicals
to warn the others

they share nutrients
through their roots

a secret language
of respect for their neighbors

an ancient network
of living beings

interconnected compassion
speaking without words

all beneath our feet.

BUD

MONDAY-MORNING SURPRISE

On my way to school
a curious thing.

I keep noticing
cracks in the sidewalks
dirt peeking through
and from those
thin lines of
earth on slabs
pieces of life pop out.

A white dandelion.
A yellow daisy.
Little pink flowers
whose name I don't know.
Even weeds. Living things.
Passed over by people
with wide strides,
too busy to notice
these flowers
finding their way
growing exactly
where they are.

Gently I pluck
a dandelion
careful its seeds
don't blow
but a push of wind

scatters its fuzz
sending seeds flying,
making their way
to new

homes.

ONE LAST THING

The first bell hasn't rung yet
but in the garden I see
people
Amy, Bill, Melissa,
and Mrs. Kapoor, too,
all gathered.

I can't wait to tell them
the new plan.

But as I near
my friends' faces
look confused
our teacher's
looks concerned.

       What happened?

Mrs. Kapoor's brow
furrows deep.

Isabel, I'm glad you're here.
I was looking for you four.
I'm so sorry, kids.
There's no easy way to say this
but the district has decided
to turn this space into something
new.
Principal Riggs
informed me this morning.

I look to my friends.
Their faces have fallen.
I don't understand.

Mrs. Kapoor says
They plan to place
portables on this space
as new classrooms
after the holiday break.
I'm heartbroken, kids.
But I had no idea.
I was just given the news.

We've already done so much work!
says Amy.

Mrs. Kapoor looks around,
walks and talks
about how we can
transfer pots
take the planters apart
find a different spot
maybe start Garden Club again
next year.
　　　　Next year?

The bell rings.
We'll figure it out.
She tries to smile.
Everyone get to class, please.

My friends' jaws drop
My eyes go straight to the

Jasmine
        Sampaguita

looking more green now
because it had finally found its
new roots, fresh start

this whole garden
dotted with buds
beginning to blossom
sprouting everywhere
with
potential
prospects
promises

turning into
another garden
where I'll have to say

goodbye.

WHAT? WAS? THAT?

says Bill.

That is. So. Not. Fair!
says Melissa.
And what about our new plan?
she says to me.

Luckily, we can keep going
next year, like Mrs. Kapoor said
says Amy.

> *We've come too far*
> *to give up now*
> is what I say.

I show them the dandelion
plucked from a crack
and how if it can
bloom through cement
so can this garden.

I share the idea Melissa and I
came up with for the
senior center fundraiser
and Lolo Frank.

Isabel, you heard Mrs. Kapoor
says Amy.

> *But what if we can convince the school*
> *not to take the garden back?*

What if we
show them
what a garden can be?

Melissa gives a grin.
What's your plan now?

In my head it seems so simple.
Out loud it's more complicated.

They step toward me
listen closely.
I plan it all on the spot
gushing out

      going with it.

All three say

Maybe.

ONE MORE PIECE

Before lunch ends
I explain to Mrs. Kapoor
our last-ditch effort
our one more try
our nothing-to-lose plan
to keep the garden going
and more importantly
why.

She drums her fingers
on her desk.

You'd have to do it soon.
The district is moving ahead.

> *I understand.*
> *We'll do it this weekend.*
> *All we ask is that you bring*
> *Principal Riggs*
> *and anyone else*
> *this might make a difference to.*
> *And if it doesn't work*
> *if we can't convince them*
> *we'll stop.*

It's her drumming that stops now.

You kids have one week.
I'll see what I can do.

YOU'RE INVITED

Putting a plan into motion means
revving the gears
keeping them going
starting, not stopping
keep going, keep moving
asking Uncle if he can donate paint
asking Plant Lady for donations
leading to donations from her Plant People Friends
getting a story placed in the paper (go Amy!)
getting a local news crew to the senior center (go Brandi!)
gathering our friends, rallying for help
keeping on with the baking
sprinkling our ideas wherever the wind takes them

and printing up flyers that announce:

NEWS! NEWS!

You Are   Cordially

Invited to Attend Bayview

Middle School's Very First

OPEN GARDEN DAY

Join Us to Support the Asian

American Senior Center

Bring Your Hearts

Your Donations

Your Time

You

!

ONE LAST INVITE

Mama sits on the couch
puffy-eyed, tired smile.
She smooths back her hair
but as soon as she sees me
her face lights up and
something inside me does, too.

Maybe, finally
she can go to an event
even though I know
she's so busy at work
making our lives better
like always.

I take my chance.

> I helped start
> the school garden
> for us. Since we
> don't have one
> here.
> At least not yet.

Mama opens her mouth
about to say
something
then stops.
Great.
But now I notice her eyes
—they're watering.

Are you okay?
Did I do something
. . . wrong?

She shakes her head.
All my years away
missing everything.
Happy and sad
when Lola sent pictures.
Happy but nervous
you'd have a hard time
here.
But, my Isa,
you've worked so hard
staying strong
making friends
finding your way.
And it's all
come from
here.
From
you.

Her finger points to
my head
my heart.

You are amazing.
I'm so proud.
Of course I'll go.
A garden!
I can't wait.

THE MORE I KNOW

For one week
two clubs
plunge ahead
bouncing between
a morning garden
a lunchtime kitchen.

My grandparents always said
cooking and gardening
go exactly together.

The more we do this
the more I see
this can work.
I just wish
we had a sign
that it will.

A GIFT

I grab a watering can
travel the pots
tipping the water.

> *Nice work, Mr. Prickles*
> I say to a cactus
> a kid brought in.
> *Looking good, Jazzy II*
> I say to the jasmine
> that's thriving.

More water, more care
my voice, my words
giving showers of love.

That's when I see
in a planter
poking out
trying hard
to reach for the sun
something green
barely there

> but *there.*

A small sprout.

I pull out a Popsicle stick
marked with Sharpie.

> *Look! Everyone!* I say.

My friends
gather, hover.

        Which seed grew?

Bill grabs the stick

        California Poppy

We smile.

Our sign.

MORNING BULLETIN!

Our teacher calls out
for a reader
and Marcus rises as if
it's his official job now
but Mrs. Kapoor surprises him
by walking past
and handing the sheet
to me.

Would you like to read today, Isabel?

Slowly
I slide up to the front
read the regular stuff
then finally
proudly
(accent and all)
get to the good part.

> *This Saturday*
> *the Garden Club and*
> *Culinary Club are hosting*
> *an Open Garden and Bake Sale*
> *for the Asian American Senior Center.*
> *Meet at the garden at eleven a.m.*
> *for friends and fun*
> *cookies and calamansi bars*
> *baked by the Culinary Club.*
> *Students may receive*

> *extra credit, please inquire*
> *with your homeroom teacher.*

It was Mrs. Kapoor who added
the extra credit part.

As I sit down Marcus whispers
Dude. Calamansi bars?
I'm there.

CALIFORNIA POPPY

The state's flower.

Long-stemmed
four-petaled
sunset-toned or
cream in the wild.
Bright orange
blanketing fields
in a superbloom.
On cloudy days
and at night
they close.
For best results
grow them in
full sun
sun the color of gold.
If they find their way
where they're planted
they'll disperse their seeds
and sprout
year after year after year.

GARDEN PARTY TIME!

I say to Mama

>   Let's go.

She looks at her watch.

Isa, can you go first
and I'll meet you?

I stand in the doorway
backpack slung on
ready to fly.

>   *Why?*

I'm waiting for someone.
Your Auntie Delia.

>   *The travel agent?*

She nods.

>   *The last time you said*
>   *you'd meet me*
>   *you never showed up.*

I just need a few minutes
to take care of something.

A knock.
Mama answers.
Why, hello, ladies!
Cora, thanks for making time.

Auntie Delia reaches
into her purse for
a large envelope.

I thought these tickets
were too important
not to drop off personally.
Shall we review?

Tickets?

What for?

She and Auntie
dive into the envelope.

        Are you coming?

Give me five minutes.

        Fine, I say
        and I wait. But
        it's taking so long.

I can't with this.

I grab my stuff
out the door
into
cool sun
soft light
swift streets
for once
my turn
to leave.

TRY AGAIN

One of her garden goodbyes
we'd spent the morning
planting bulbs
setting roots.
She'd brought
spades, seeds
snacks, smiles
and wanted
like Lolo
to teach me things.

But
how could I listen
knowing she'd be leaving
knowing whatever we'd plant
might not go
as planned?

Because
gardens don't
always go your way
no matter how much
water or sun
or love you give.

There could be pests, disease
too much sun
too much water
or not enough.

So I'd hoped today
we'd erase that memory
by making a new one.
I'd hoped today
would give us
our chance
to try again.

But
all this work
for nothing.

OLD AND NEW

Both clubs meet at
our garden-in-progress.

Let's get moving!
Bill says
and Amy pulls out
the school's decoration bins.

To dress up our garden
we drape Tibetan flags
from pole to pole
and send prayers of
goodwill on the wind.
We shake out
flowered tablecloths.
We pull out sparkly ornaments
from a box marked *Holiday*
so that even the calamansi tree
gets a colorful treatment
of shimmery trinkets.

> In the Philippines
> Christmas starts
> as early as September
> lingering until December
> full of feasts and neighbors.
> Parols get hung in windows
> —star-shaped lanterns
> made from paper and bamboo

that shimmer in the day
and glow brightly at night
a reminder of family and
of light over darkness

I hang every bright bulb
on all the garden's trees
and realize I have
here and now
to remind me
of old and new
of hope and wonder
of two homes at once.

WE'RE READY

Some parents have
come early to help
but still
no Mama.

My hands buzz
thinking of her
not coming
again.
It's all I want today.

Melissa watches me
watching the gate
and thankfully says

Look at the tables!

She's right.
Topped with treats
gloves, tools
plants, pots
—all of it donated from
friends, businesses.
Makes me forget
for a moment.

Because
The best part?
My club friends
turned real friends
here
waiting, ready.

SOON

Auntie and Uncle arrive.
More parents and students
many of the seniors.
Lola Yoling with Lolo Frank
both all grins.

Every person
chatting
eating
buying
gardening
enjoying
this sun-filled day
enjoying
what we've created
and what we're
creating.

I scan the gate.
No sign of her.
But can't worry now
since the people
we need
have arrived.

Mrs. Kapoor
with our principal
Mrs. Riggs
charge our way.

GIVE IT MY ALL

You ready? Amy asks.

> *Been practicing all week.*

They approach
We approach
We meet
in the middle.
I lay out our case.

How we can get Garden Club started again.
How this garden can bring students and seniors together
again.
How we can use what we grow here
—in so many different ways.
For our classes, for the school.
For learning, for giving back.

> *All we ask is the chance to*
> *keep going, to*
> *keep growing.*

We want this to be
a community garden
says Melissa.
We want to open it to everyone.
Bring the old programs back
but make them new.

The school
the seniors

our neighborhood
says Bill.

Amy says
We've scouted the school
this is the best spot
the best sun and shade
the perfect spot to keep it.
We've done all the prep.

Just look around
at all these people
excited
to make this space their own
says Melissa.

Kids, says our principal
—I'm impressed.
But it's not up to me, ultimately.
Let me think about this
and talk to the district.
We will keep you posted.

Bill says
While you're here
have a calamansi bar!
(He grins at me.)

Mrs. Kapoor says
No matter what happens
you've done
amazing work.

We'll get a garden
here or elsewhere.
You've planted the seed.
Great job, everyone.

Amy grabs two shovels
and extends them
to Mrs. Kapoor and Principal Riggs,
the garden's fate
in their actual hands.

SHE STILL HASN'T COME

Around the garden people enjoy
the smell of earth
sunlight on their faces
the richness of soil.

I need to stop
watching the gate.
She's not coming.

Gardens can give
the deepest joy or
the deepest sorrow.
I've had both.
Unpredictable
uncontrollable
unwieldy in their weeds
so that all you can give
back to your garden is
patience.
Lolo taught me that.

There's a pit
in my stomach
but even with
my heart heavy
I get working.

She's still not here.

UNTIL

Melissa nudges me
and nods toward
the gate.
That's when I see

Mama made it.

She comes over
pulls on gloves
gets to work
by my side
in time for Mrs. Kapoor
to ask, so kindly:

Who is this lovely person
you've brought with you today,
Isabel?

I introduce my mother
for the very first time.

BEFORE WE LEAVE

We all take a quick photo
for my grandparents this time.
Lolo will love seeing this
whether it stays or gets moved.

BLOOM

IT'S A DATE

The next morning
I wake and see
Mama was right.
This apartment has
beautiful natural light
pooling my room.

Mama knocks
peeks in.

Get out of bed, Sleepyhead
Time for our Date Night!
Or Date Day
I should say?
I've been dreaming of
clam chowder . . .

SHE HAS THE WHOLE DAY PLANNED

We venture into the depths
of Fisherman's Wharf.

Pier 39
feels wet
sounds loud
smells fishy.

We grab two steaming-hot cups
a thick, creamy soup
a bench to sit and sip
and people-watch.

She wants to see things
we haven't seen yet
together
so after chowder
we venture out
to find Lombard Street.

THE CROOKEDEST STREET IN THE WORLD

Lombard Street
             is lined with
                 fancy houses
                  and paved with
               old red bricks
       that twist and turn
whip and wind
      zig and zag
            up and down.
              Legend calls it
                 the crookedest street
                   in the world
             (even though that's
       actually Vermont Street
—also in San Francisco)
     but it's fine
         because this
              precarious
                 pivoting path
           is enough to
       make me forget
      why I was
    ever mad about
leaving there
    for here
      at all.

LAST STOP

The city mixes with green
life weaving its way onto
cement and sidewalks
flowers coming up in cracks
trees lining curbs
streets that end in parks
like the one in front of us
now.

THE BOTANICAL GARDEN

Your lolo told me to take you here.

    Just like in his tourist book.

We smile at each other.

The botanical garden
in the middle of
Golden Gate Park
has a thousand shades of green
and flowers in every color.

These things fill me
but it's this walk
breathing in
watching everything
keeping together
this whole day that
makes me feel good
about this place
less doubtful
about this city
more sure
of who I am
so far away from home.

Because I'm starting to see
signs of home
everywhere.

Familiar spots
faces no longer so foreign
—like Mama's.

And I'm starting to see
that maybe
I only needed to
start
with her.

WE STROLL

There's still
one thing
for me
to know.

> *Are you going back to New York?*

We pause.

People and plants
all around.

I breathe. Explain.

> *The calls*
> *the clues*
> *then Auntie Delia came by.*
> *She said "tickets."*
> *I'm sorry I didn't tell you*
> *about any of that stuff.*
> *I got worried that*
> *you'd leave me again.*

Mama stares.

> *Is that what's happening?*
> *You're leaving me?*

Mama points.

A bench.

We sit.

From her purse an

envelope.

OPEN IT

Envelopes and boxes.
My mother's ways.

I lift the flap.
Two sets of plane tickets.
Two names.
Ours.
One set to New York.
Another set to Manila.
Both sets fly back to
San Francisco.

    What?

Finally we'll visit New York together
during Christmas break.
We'll do all the fun things
we always talked about.
Just me and you.

    Will there be snow?

Maybe!
Then over summer break
we'll go home
to visit your lolo and lola.
Definitely no snow there
she laughs, then looks at me
seriously.

I'm not leaving you anymore, my Isa.

Mama.

I wrap my arms around her.

My mother
my first country
My mother
my first home.

MONDAY MORNING'S NEWS (AS ANNOUNCED BY MARCUS)

Since the school liked our display
of students leading the way
and the ideas we made flow
—the garden gets to grow!

SUMMER BREAK

My new room
filled with
plants and light
filled with friends
Melissa and Brandi
who help me get ready
for my trip with Mama
before summer break ends.

On my desk sit
three snow globes.

The first, New York
Mama's original gift.

The second, San Francisco
a Golden Gate Bridge
swirled up in glittery snow,
which seems funny to me now.
I've gotten to know that
fall is hot
summers, foggy
but never snowflakes.

The third, New York
from my visit over winter
where we tried ice-skating
saw all the lights and snow
climbed stairs to the top

of the Empire State Building.
I even met her nanny family.
Weird, definitely
but Nicolette gave me a hug
then we all spent the day
strolling through
city and gardens and
I saw how in their own way
they love my mother, too.

Brandi shakes up
all three globes
as I zip up my suitcase
and Melissa
bored from my bed
says

Let's go do something.

HOME

We make our way
down hilly streets
gabbing
and soon
we're near school.

*Hey, I know
let's go check on our garden*
says Melissa.

We've done this all summer
sometimes with seniors
our little routine.

Brandi sprints ahead.
So does Melissa.

> *Hey, wait up!*

and they do
and we laugh
and we run.

I USED TO NOT KNOW WHAT TO DO

We enter our space
the metal fence clanging open
the sign still there

School Garden. All Are Welcome.

Buds and blooms
in varying states
with so much green
and vibrant pops of color.

We know what to do
traveling the fence with the hose
yanking weeds when we see them
Saying hello to our plant friends.
Melissa and Brandi use
funny voices like a comedy routine

What's up, Leaf-onardo DiCaprio! (A fern.)
Lookin' sharp, Mr. Prickles! (A cactus.)
Thyme for some fertilizer, Powerpuff Girls! (A cluster of herbs.)

My friends crack themselves up.

I think about
Jazzy, my sampaguita
back home, once wilted.
How I left her like that
not knowing what to do
before leaving.

I used to not know what to do.
How to picture myself here
How to spot the familiar
How to truly
hold on and let go.

But now?
It's different.
Roots launched.

Among a bed of
veggies-to-be
I notice
a dandelion
poking up and out.
Its fuzzy head
perfectly symmetrical.

I pluck it
blow softly
watch the fuzz
float away
on the wind,
no longer wondering
where the seeds
will land.

HOW SEEDS ARE CARRIED

A few days before I left
for California
I asked my grandfather
how flowers can grow
in unlikely places
like up through
cracks in cement.
He said

Have you ever blown
on a dandelion
and watched the seeds
float away on the wind?

Some seeds
have wings.

They're light
with feathery bristles
and get dispersed
where the breeze goes.
They travel far by flight
fluttering to the ground
finding their place
spreading
rooting
sprouting
growing
finding water

turning up to the sun
budding

then blossoming

wherever
they are
planted.

A seed always finds
its way, anak.
And when it's ready,
in its own time,
it will

bloom.

HELLOS LOOK LIKE

Summer in my small town
green hills and rice fields
Cristina, Rosamie, and I
running into one giant hug.

We Missed You sounds like
them telling me everything and anything
how we've finally turned thirteen
how we feel different and the same.

Good days taste like
the calamansi cupcakes I've baked.
I hand one to Lolo, Lola, and Mama
we bite into the sweet and the sour.

Home smells like
rows of sampaguita
perfuming the air with their
thick lush musk.

Hello is
Lola's bright smile
the rising sun
the sweetness still on my tongue
and my heart spotting
everything familiar
but noticing that
still, somehow
it feels almost like new.

WHEREVER I'M PLANTED

I walk with my grandfather
through
a thousand shades of green
      plants dressed in dew
      flowers flooded in light
as birds fill the trees with their
wild loud songs.
Our garden
comes alive
in mornings.

Lolo drags a hose
the water trickling slow
pausing at
an empty planter.

My beloved

Jasmine
      Sampaguita

Gone.

I crouch to the spot
where I first planted Jazzy.
Did she not make it?

He lays the hose
on a vegetable patch
and says

Come, my Isa, I have a surprise.

He leads me to
a large pot, a single shrub

Jasmine
          Sampaguita

I grin at him.

          Is this what I think it is?

Yep! The one you planted
remember? I thought
I sent you a picture.
It grew!
So I moved it.
They can survive
anywhere, you know.
And look

Next to it
another planter of
different flowers of
deep golden petals.

The California poppy seeds
you sent. Good choice, anak.
They can grow anywhere, too,
Just need a good spot
some good sun.

I crouch down.

>*You made it*
>I whisper to them
>as if they're my friends
>almost expecting replies.

Neither has a full
bed of blooms yet
just enough
to glimpse their strength
to see what's possible.

DAY BREAKS

Guess what?
Lolo grins.
I have more seeds.
Old ones, new ones.
Shall we plant some
after breakfast?

He promised we'd plant.
I promised I'd make
ube meringue pancakes.
(Yum.)

       Sure. I smile back.

Lolo lifts the hose
and off he whistles.

All around
sunlight pours in
casting shadows
making the light
shift.

Some of the flowers
get full sun
while others get
needed shade from
generous trees.

The light fans over rows of

Jasmine
Sampaguita

and lands on
my own little plant
still here
surviving, thriving
following the light.
Still here
giving, receiving
resilient like me.

All around
I smell earth
I feel warmth
I see possibilities.
And
I see now, how
I've always known
what to do.
Like everything I've
planted this year
I've found my place
I've spread my roots
And now
I turn my face
to the sun
and I

bloom.

AUTHOR'S NOTE

About writing the book

Like many Filipino American kids, I grew up with a cherished ritual. My mom would set up a giant cardboard box, the words *balikbayan box* printed on the side, and I'd help her fill it with things for our extended family—such as clothes and household goods, and pretty shades of lipstick for my aunties (which I would beg my mom to try, though she always said no). A special freight service would pick it up and off it would go, thousands of miles from California to the Philippines.

The history of the balikbayan box goes back to the 1970s, when staggering unemployment rates in the Philippines forced many Filipinos to leave their families and find work in other countries. Those boxes became bridges. They were a reminder of sacrifices made, connecting families across oceans with messages of love.

The symbolism of this box—along with a girl and a garden—were the seeds that helped me begin writing Isabel's story. I wanted to explore how we long for and find home, the complexities of mother-daughter relationships, and how young people can build and support communities—all centered around fun, awesome kids who find out they have the power to grow their own ideas.

When I first started brainstorming, something else that was weighing on my mind was the ongoing targeted violence against Asian American elders, which I eventually wove into the book. It was important to me for Isabel and her friends to empathize with, learn from, and honor the generations who came before her. After much tending to all of these threads, what came out was Isabel's tender, resilient, and hopeful journey of spreading her roots in a new home.

About growing a poetry garden

Isabel in Bloom is a novel in verse, which means it's written entirely in poems. Using poetic elements like rhythm, symbolism, and repetition helped me to find the novel's heart.

Writing this book was a bit like gardening. I took every poem one step at a time, giving each one love and care, until I had a poetry garden of varying textures and lengths and tones. The majority of poems in this book are written in free verse, but I also used other forms, such as:

> **acrostic:** A poem in which the first letter of each line spells out a name, word, or phrase when read vertically. ("Meet the Cousins," page 92)
>
> **free verse:** This format has no particular rhyming structure. The poet makes the rules. ("Dinner Advice," page 27)
>
> **haiku:** A type of poem that comes from Japan. The format has three lines, with five syllables in the first line, seven syllables in the second line, and five syllables in the third line. ("Caution," page 274)
>
> **narrative:** This poem tells an overarching story, much like a novel. It is typically longer than other forms of poetry ("My Favorite Memory," page 68)
>
> **palindrome:** A palindromic poem, or mirrored poem, reads the same backward and forward. ("Mirror Mirror," page 214)

tanaga: An indigenous Filipino poetry form. Traditionally, the tanaga was written in Tagalog and untitled. It consists of four lines (a quatrain) with seven syllables per line, and the same rhyme at the end of each line. Modern tanagas can use different combinations of rhyme schemes; I experimented a bit with the format, so the tanaga poems in this book are not all traditional in nature. ("There to Here," page 51)

visual or concrete: This type of poem creates a visual image related to its meaning. ("The Crookedest Street in the World," page 337)

I hope this book inspires you to learn more about poetry—and to have fun writing your own! Just remember: there's no right or wrong way to write poetry. It's about the joy of playing with words, reading them aloud, and listening to the language roll and the melody sing.

Here are a few prompts based on Isabel's story to help you grow your own poetry garden:

1. When Isabel meets her cousins for the first time, we discover more about them through their names. Describe a friend as an acrostic poem. ("Meet the Cousins," page 92)

2. Isabel and her mom ship balikbayan boxes home to their family and friends in the Philippines to show their love. Write a poem about what you'd pack in your own box. Who would you send it to? What items would you include? ("Her First Visit Home," page 63)

3. Look in the mirror and write a palindrome poem describing what you see. ("Mirror Mirror," page 214)

4. Isabel's mother, Cora, does a very hard thing—she leaves her family in order to give them a better life. Write a poem about something hard that you or a loved one has done. ("No Going Back," page 252)

5. Isabel is nervous on the first day of her new school. Write a poem about your first day of school. Try to detail what you're noticing around you, and also what you're feeling inside. ("First Day" page 99)

6. Isabel meets and becomes friends with people at her local senior center. Write a poem about an older person in your life, or an older person you want to meet. ("The Next Morning," page 293)

7. Many of the poems in this novel use the five senses, such as when Isabel's in her garden or during her culinary adventures. Write a poem using details, images, or symbolism around all five senses: sight, sound, taste, touch, and feel. ("Hellos Look Like," page 352)

ACKNOWLEDGMENTS

Just like a garden, this book received a lot of love and tending by way of many, *many* (!) words read aloud, in order to make it bloom. Sending my gratitude to those who gave their time and thoughts to Isabel's story:

My lovely editor, Dana Carey, who not only helped grow this book with her brilliance, care, and deep insight, but who also helped me grow as a writer through every iteration of Isabel's story.

Wendy Lamb for her thoughtful eye, warm cheerleading, and continued support.

Illustrator Gica Tam and art director Jade Rector for this book's rich, delightful cover, and Cathy Bobak for the gorgeous interior design. Copyeditors Barbara Perris and Colleen Fellingham for their expert eyes. And managing editor Tamar Schwartz for keeping us on track.

Amazing though now retired agent, Sarah Davies, for her help on this book, and Chelsea Eberly for taking over—and my wonderful agent, Jennifer Laughran, for her guidance as I keep on this publication journey.

Early readers Christina Newhard and Ella deCastro Baron for their nuanced reflections.

The wonderful Random House Children's Books School and Library team, who have been instrumental in helping connect my books to educators and young readers . . . and for all the fun event signings, dinners, and schmoozing!

My husband, Mark, who helps nurture our family life. Our boys, Alden and Cael, who support Writer-Mom in their own ways, and who are blossoming into incredible young men.

To our dog, Riggs—aka Riggsarooney, Biggzabooney, Fangers, Belly Boi, Coyote Killa—for lending his name to one of the minor characters in this book (did you spot it?!) and for being the sweet, snarly buddy who got me out for walks when my revision-eyes were going bonkers.

And finally, to you, the reader! I hope this book sparks your own journey in realizing how resilient you are, asking questions about those who came before you, and maybe even growing your own poetry garden. Thank you for spending time with this book. xx

ABOUT THE AUTHOR

MAE RESPICIO writes middle-grade novels full of heart and hope, including *The House That Lou Built,* which won an Asian/Pacific American Libraries Association Honor award and was an NPR Best Book. Some of Mae's dearest childhood memories are of spending time in each of her lolas' rich, lush gardens. She's currently working on her green thumb.

To say hello and learn more about Mae's books, visit her at maerespicio.com.